The Lost Princess of Abbigonia

The Barbarian Invasion

By
Mark Peanut Three Accola

Illistrations
Stephen Accola

Mark Accola
133 81st Avenue North
Saint Petersburg, FL 33702
www.peanutthree.com

Book Layout © 2017 BookDesignTemplates.com

The Lost Princess of Abbigonia/ Mark Peanut Three Accola. -- 1st ed.
ISBN 978-0-0000000-0-0

Mark Peanut Three Accola

For Mimi,
the first person to read my book

Ten soldiers led wisely will beat a hundred without a head.

–EURIPIDES

The Lost Princess of Abbigonia

Contents

Mark Peanut Three Accola

The Castle Siege

I t was high noon and the sun shined brightly in the sky on one side of the mountains. A few dark clouds blocked the sun's rays and darkened the peaceful snow-covered mountains on the other side. A cave halfway down the mountain was dark and decrepit. As a small rock fell from the top of the cave and onto the cave's floor, there was the sound of something large that had just stirred. Glowing red eyes appeared in the darkness and puffs of smoke curled upwards in a series of huffs. A dragon with cobweb-covered wings and scales so ancient they had grayed from age took a few steps out of the cave and narrowed his eyes as he came into the light. He took a few short breaths as he slowly woke up, small flames shooting from his nostrils. The dragon stepped out of the darkness of the cave, leaned back on his hindquarters, and stretched out his front legs, dust falling off his body, before lightly shaking his head back and forth. He lightly flapped his wings and shook his massive bulk, dust and dirt falling from his body, creating a cloud of dust. Now fully awake, the dragon took a few deep breaths, smoke filling the air. Then, in one long exhale, fire erupted from his mouth.

Extending his wings, the dragon began to run down the mountain. As he flapped his wings, he started to lift off the ground. Just before he reached the bottom of the mountain, he flapped his wings one final time and took off. Giving a few large and labored flaps, he lifted above the tree line. A scream echoed through the mountains, and suddenly the dragon disappeared into the clouds. The black outline of his body only just visible, and then it slowly became more defined when suddenly he burst through the clouds.

The sound of explosions, burning wood, and the clanking of metal on metal filled the air as the dragon flew past the trees and over a giant castle in the middle of a walled city being burnt to the ground. As the dragon looked down on the scene below him, he could hear the terror and desperation ravaging the city's streets. He looked at the battle and saw the grim situation of the defending army as the barbarians savagely climbed over the walls and cut a path through the middle of the already burning town.

As the dragon circled, he looked at the people in the town and saw a young girl gazing at the diamond necklaces in the window of a jewelry store, oblivious to the happenings around her as her teacher tried to tug her away and protect her from the battle.

A familiar gleam of red hair not too far from the girl caught his eye. Captain Ruhk, leader of the armies of Abbigonia, was giving orders to a small crowd of soldiers. The dragon watched as Captain Ruhk clenched his shield tightly and began frantically waving his sword around, barking out commands as his soldiers scrambled around and tried to fight off the imminent invasion. He had scars mixed with tattoos on his arms and his armor was tattered and worn. Captain Ruhk's hazel eyes and red hair gleamed in the sun as he saw the dragon flying over head and headed toward the castle. A messenger Ran up to Captain Ruhk and pointed toward the castle. The dragon spied a warehouse and townsfolk who carried random weapons, armor, and books out the building. He also saw people trying to flee to their homes, seeking shelter from the invading army of brutish barbarians.

Flying up into the sky, the dragon showed the full span of his wings, and flew high enough to be missed by arrows and spells alike. Commotion by the city wall caught his attention where he saw King Tentaclous and his second in command, the boorish Captain Clod, charge into the middle of the battle, loving every minute of it. Confident in his victory King Tentaclous hadn't even put his armor on. The dragon huffed, letting small tendrils of smoke curl from his nostrils.

3

The Lost Princess of Abbigonia

Flying faster than before, he turned towards the castle. Surrounded by a wall with small towers beside each of its gates, it sat higher than the rest of the city with grand wooden doors in the middle that opened when the dragon neared. The dragon flew in and landed with a heavy thump on the marble flooring of the huge throne room where the King and Queen were fighting alongside the royal guards; it seemed the barbarians were everywhere. Letting out an almighty roar, the dragon enveloped the room in fire, forcing the barbarians to run in all directions. The air cleared, revealing the Queen's protective shell shielding herself, the King and the royal guards. The King smiled and stood up to meet his friend with open arms. Sadness could be seen on his middle-aged face as he smiled and welcomed his old friend. The Queen, elegant and strong, stood next to the king with a glowing pendant around her neck that radiated a bright red light.

The Lost Princess of Abbigonia

"Welcome home, Tarragon, how comes our defense?" asked the king, already knowing the inevitable truth.

"My Queen, my Liege, I wish I could bring more fair tidings but we have precious little time. There is a barbarian army at your gates, larger than anything we have seen before. At my age, even if we fight, we will still loose," replied the old dragon.

"I see." The King turned to one of the royal guards. "Soldier, I need you to go and get Captain Ruhk. We've got to prepare the army."

"Is there enough time?" asked the Queen.

"She's right, we have to make preparations for the-" Tarragon suddenly paused mid-sentence.

"-for the Princess and the royal pendant," said the Queen.

"Will you take the child and watch over her? Can you make sure she knows of her heritage and is strong enough to reclaim her right one day, "Asked the King.

"Will you give her this when she is old enough?" asked the Queen as she took the pendant from around her neck and reached out to hand it to the dragon, when the King suddenly grabbed.

"No, we must hide it, with a message to the people to not lose hope. That one day the true queen will return and take back what is rightfully hers," proclaimed the King with a proud look on this face.

The doors to the room burst open and Captain Ruhk and the guard ran towards them. "My Lord, there is an army at our gates and our soldiers are overwhelmed, I need to get back out there." A soldier appeared behind the Captain, escorting Princess Tiara who ran up to the Queen, tears streaming down her face.

The king looked down at his daughter a moment and then looked back to Captain Ruhk with his decision. "Take this and get out of the city." He roughly handed the pendant to the Captain, closing his fist around the jewel as its light faded. "And spread the message that one day the true queen will return and this pendant will glow a bright red when she does," said the King.

"Sir, I can't leave my men, I belong out there with them," demanded Captain Ruhk.

"You can and will as a direct order from me," said the King sternly.

Captain Ruhk paused a moment before replying. "I know just the person to give it to for safekeeping. She is nine years old, and she is fixated with jewelry."

"Will a girl that young be able to keep it safe?" asked the Queen.

"The girl you are speaking of, does she have black hair?" asked Tarragon.

"Yes," replied Captain Ruhk.

"I think I saw her when I flew in; she was gazing at some jewelry," said Tarragon. "What of the girl's parents? The girl would be in considerable danger."

"I'm her father. I always hoped she would be interested in learning the sword," said Captain Ruhk.

"I'm sure she'll come around. When you think people aren't paying attention, most of the time they are," said the King.

"Wishing you had a boy, perhaps?" said Tarragon.

Captain Ruhk chuckles softly, "No, I suppose not."

"Keep it safe, will you? It may be the only thing her parents can give her," said the Queen.

"I give you my word, my queen. I will die protecting it," said Captain Ruhk.

The King cleared his throat and then looked down at his own daughter. "My daughter and the hope of my people, know that your mother and I love you very much. My queen, you can go with the dragon there's no need for you to die too," said the King.

"I'm not going anywhere without you, my king, my love," said the Queen.

"King Tentaclous might know that you had a wife, my king. If the Queen came with me, he might be inclined to search for her and possibly your daughter." There was a pause as this sunk in as everyone in the room started to hear screams and cries in pain as the battle outside raged on and became more and more one sided towards the barbarians. "I'm sorry but it's time," said Tarragon.

"And so it is, dragon. I hope we see each other again. My King, my Queen, it has been my greatest honor," said Captain Ruhk before quickly leaving through one of the side exits.

"Fair well and good luck to you both," said the King holding back tears to Tarragon and Tiara. Tarragon nodded and placed the princess on his back. Then he turned and ran toward the main entrance. Kicking the large throne room doors open, he breathed a large blow of fire which sent several barbarians running. He then jumped up, stretched his wings and flew high into the sky, quickly disappearing behind the clouds.

"Are you sure she'll be safe?" asked the worried Queen.

"I can think of no other being that could take better care of her," said the King.

The barbarians kept pouring into the city. King Tentaclous entered the castle along with so many of his army it made it hard to walk through the throne room. The barbarians cuffed and enslaved the servants and warriors of the old king. The King and Queen lovingly gazed into each other's eyes one last time until the Barbarian King walked up, his men forming a circle around them. The King and Queen dropped their weapons.

"Your armies have fallen, old king. Not even a dragon would face me. The Great Kingdom of Abbigonia has been erased from the world. It is a shame you are too weak to understand real strength, even when it stands before you," said King Tentaclous before laughing a deep booming laugh.

"True power is when your rule goes unquestioned, even when you're not there," said the old King. "Old man, such snide comments will only hasten your death, and will do nothing to prevent them," said King Tentaclous. "As the future can do nothing to prevent your death," stated the Queen.

"One day the walls of justice will close in around you and your sins will catch up to you," said the old king.

"That day will never come by your people. Know that your tiny kingdom won't be the only one to fall. All the kingdoms, everywhere, will fall to the might of my armies," cried King Tentaclous.

"At the cost of how many lives? How many have you killed already?" shouted the Queen.

"More than you will ever know," King Tentaclous stated proudly. Drawing his sword, the new king swiftly ran them through, giving first the Queen and then the King a mercifully quick death.

Chapter II

Ruhk's Escape

Captain Ruhk ran through the burning town, dodging collapsing buildings and attacking the occasional barbarian warrior that came across him with a quick parry and thrust before moving on. He soon came to a small hut with a straw roof, which was on fire and blazing wildly. Crashing through the now fragile door, he saw his daughter hiding in the smoke-filled corner of the main room. Running to her, Captain Ruhk called, "Crystal, we have to go."

"My doll caught fire!" said Crystal in a soft smoke-filled voice.

Picking up his soot-covered daughter, Captain Ruhk said, "I'll get you a new one. Come on, child, we have to leave now."

Just then part of the roof caved in. Red-hot embers started to fall on top of them. Captain Ruhk held onto his daughter, keeping her tight against his chest and, thinking quickly, ran and jumped out of the window. He landed on his back which knocked the wind from his lungs and it took him a moment to recover.

"Poppy, are you alright?" Crystal asked, tears beginning to form in her eyes from the shock.

Captain Ruhk gasped for air as he stood up. "Let's go," he said. Before they could take a step, barbarians ambushed them who were looting and enslaving the town and its people. With no time to try to fight them this time, he picked up his daughter again and started to run through the town.

He dodged a barbarian's blade, and another's huge mace. He ran and jumped through a house that burned as he got closer and closer to a crumbled break in the city wall. He ran under a building supported by burning pillars which was going to crumble at any moment only to be stopped by the boorish Captain Clod. Clod swung his bloody spiked mace.

"Weak, pathetic humans, so easily crushed. Stop running and I'll show you," he sneered. Captain Clod stood facing Captain Ruhk wearing tattered armor as if he had been in a hundred battles already. The horde that had followed Captain Ruhk through the streets appeared round the corner just as Clod delivered the first swing. Still holding onto his daughter, Captain Ruhk dodged the swing and watched as it knocked out a burning pillar. Suddenly hit by an idea, Captain Ruhk ran between barbarians, creating chaos and confusion as they each tried to grab at him only to end up hitting each other. He reappeared on the other side of the rabble in front of the other pillar.

Clod swung his mace at his own men, forcing them out of his way. Aiming at Captain Ruhk, Clod swung again, missed and knocked out the other pillar, forcing the whole platform down on top of them. Dodging the blow, Captain Ruhk cleared the crumbling structure before it came crashing down, barely making it out with Crystal.

Before the barbarians could recover, Captain Ruhk grabbed Crystal and started to move again as they ran out of the city and into the forest. Out of breath, Captain Ruhk staggered and set his daughter down, deeming it safe enough for them to walk.

"Is it my turn to carry you, poppy?" Crystal asked.

"Darling, if you could carry me, then there may be hope for this kingdom yet," he chuckled.

After they had been walking through the forest for some time, Captain Ruhk turned to Crystal and said, "I want you to take care of something for me. The King himself gave it to me himself and I need you to take care of it until his daughter comes and finds it."

"Really? What is it?" Crystal asked.

Captain Ruhk took out the royal pendant which was now clear like a diamond. Crystal's eyes widened in amazement. "For me?" she whispered.

"My daughter, one day the queen will return. When she does, the pendant will glow bright red. It will be up to you to keep it safe until she does. Can you do that?" Captain Ruhk asked, narrowing his eyes at her playfully. Crystal reached out slowly took the necklace.

"It's beautiful," she breathed.

Captain Ruhk took the pendant and slipped it over her head. "Can you do that for me?" he asked.

Crystal nodded as she gazed down at the jewel. Captain Ruhk nodded and they started to walk deeper into the forest.

"Good, I know of an abandoned farmhouse far away from here, there we can celebrate your 4th birthday." said Captain Ruhk.

"But I'll be 5 though." Crystal said.

"Oh, of course." Captain Ruhk said out of breath and keeping an eye out of more barbarians.

Chapter III

Siren's Cave

Tarragon and Princess Tiara, perched on his back, looked down at the defeated city one last time. Tarragon made for home and as they flew through the air, Tiara clenched the dragon tightly. She finally opened one eye as they flew straight and steady. She leaned back up and opened her second eye, stretching her hands up to feel the clouds pass through her fingers.

The flight to their new home was long and quiet. They final arrived at the mountain and landed on a ledge jutting out in front of a cave, behind them a steep fall down to the forest. The future queen climbed down and stayed close to the dragon as they walked into the cave together. The dragon watched the young girl for a minute, and yawned. Tiara walked around the cave, looking at the walls and in all the cracks and crevices. The dragon's eyes slowly began to close and, noticing how tired she felt, Tiara ran over and snuggled in next to him.

Tiara awakened after a while, stood up and stretched. It was then she heard something she couldn't quite figure out what it was. Curiously, she started to walk deeper into the cave. Eerie sounds played quietly in the background and the Princess heard her mother call to her. As she turned a corner, she saw her mother standing in the middle of the cave. Tiara jumped in excitement and started to run toward her. The queen then started to sing and Tiara stopped in her tracks, mesmerized.

Meanwhile Tarragon woke up and looked around, eventually calling out Tiara's name. The dragon huffed and, pulling himself to his feet, wandered deeper into the cave after her. He looked around but became more frantic in the darkness. The cave was damp and dark, with whispers that seemed to come from everywhere.

Eventually hearing singing, he followed the sound only to find Tiara hypnotized by a hideous Siren.

The dragon saw the disgusting creature's true form; a nasty, pungent woman with grey skin and scales around her knees and elbows. Angrily, he charged down the tunnel to save Tiara. Then, suddenly, a drooling, repugnant pig-man jumped out from one of the shadows of the cave.

"Reeeet, attack!" shouted the Grunting, a half-man, half-pig creature.

Stealthily, a Mudmucker, popped up from the cave floor. He was a furry, mud-covered creature with eagle-like eyes and razor sharp talons. "The tasty treat is ours, dragon!" shouted the Mudmucker and the two creatures attacked.

They clawed at the dragon, but were swept away by a powerful swipe of Tarragon's claw. Using his mouth, Tarragon grabbed one of the attackers and threw him against the wall. Meanwhile, the Siren still sung, drawing Tiara closer and closer to a cauldron bubbling away in the corner.

Tarragon rushed forward and tried to grab the child only to be held back by the Grunting. Tarragon growled with rage, and threw the Grunting and the

Mudmucker behind him. He spun around, took a deep breath and then released a huge blast of fire, forcing the Mudmucker and the Grunting from the cave.

The Siren's voice echoed within the cave as she began to help the child walk up the stones that led to the cauldron. Tarragon wrapped his tail around Tiara and pulled her back out of sight. With a confident smile, he then punted the Siren out of the cave, sending her flying. The Mudmucker and the Grunting could only watch as the Siren flew out of the cave and sailed through into the forest.

The dragon limped back to where he'd slept before and lay down

"It is my job to protect you, young Tiara. But I need you to be more careful.My name is Tarragon. I will teach you everything I have learned over these long years but for now, I need to rest"

Tiara nodded. Satisfied she was okay, Tarragon lay his head on the floor. Tiara walked over and curled up between his legs, falling asleep in a matter of seconds. Tarragon gently breathed out smoke, his eyes changing color as he focused on it, and turned it into a blanket. Gently, he covered Tiara with the blanket and lay his head down on the cave floor.

Chapter IV

Siren's Plan

Night fell over the forest. The moon and the stars shined brightly in the night sky. A flying creature soared just above the trees of the forest, taking in everything for miles. The defeated villains talked over a campfire and discussed how things could have gone better. Noctremis, part-human part-moth with luminescent wings and strange neon glowing eyes, flew down from above and met the Siren, Grunting, and.

"Reet, that stupid dragon put huge gashes in my side," said the Grunting. The Mudmucker looked around with quick and sudden movements, like that of an eagle.

"You should have seen yourself run out of the cave, Grunting," said the Mudmucker. Noctremis was behind them all in the shadows watching what was happening at the camp as the Mudmucker laughed at his own comment.

"Iii haaave neeews. King Tentaclous has taken over the kingdom and iis searching for the heir to the throne. A chiiild, most likely escorted by a dragoooon," said Noctremis.

"A dragon, eh?" said the Siren out loud, thinking to herself. The Siren looked at the campfire, her mental wheels turning as she contemplated this new knowledge.

"Hey Noc, did you see Grunting over here when we ran out of the cave?" the Mudmucker asked.

"No, I was to faaar away. What happened to you three, go up against a Gryphon or something?" asked Noctremis.

"What if we...?" the Siren mumbled to herself.

"No, actually, we just fought a dragon. Where were you? You should have been there," said the Mudmucker to Noctremis.

"He was too busy flapping around, oh look it's king Tentaclous," said the Grunting in a mocking voice.

"At least I didn't get my tail whipped. What, did he jump out and surprise you? Poor things," said Noctremis. Siren was deep in thought.

The Mudmucker stopped tending to his wounds and looked up at Noctremis. "I didn't see you run in and attack him so you don't get to mock," said Mudmucker.

"Oh, and I suppose the fact I found that cave in the first place means nothing? You two are stupid," said Noctremis.

"Reet! That's it, it's go time!" yelled the Grunting as he jumped up and tackled Noctremis.

The Mudmucker jumped up and joined in the fight just because he could. Just as the Mudmucker and Grunting were winning against Noctremis, Grunting accidently hit the Mudmucker and then they started to go at it.

"Even if they don't find the same cave, the king would reward us for such useful information. I might even earn his trust," muttered the Siren under her breath.

"Ouch, hey! Siren, help!" Noctremis called out trying to escape the fight. "Be quiet and take your lickings," said the Grunting.

"Hold his arms, I've got his feet," said the Mudmucker.

"Alright, I've got his arms. Now hit him," said the Grunting.

"My hands are tied up holding his arms, you hit him," said the Mudmucker.

"Well, I can't hit him, my hands are full holding his feet," said the Grunting. Then the Mudmucker and the Grunting looked at each other for a moment.

"Enough, you three idiots, sit down and let him go. We are leaving at dawn for King Tentaclous' army and his new keep. We will tell him about our little scrap and that we've found the dragon and little girl he is looking for. With any luck, I can manipulate my way into a nice comfy advisory position to the king," said the Siren with a crooked evil grin.

The three creatures stopped fighting, each slapping another one last time like children before sitting down. The Siren rolled her eyes and laid down for the night. Noctremis stuck his tongue out and then laid down close to the Siren with his back almost right up against hers knowing that he would be safe when he was close to her. The Mudmucker and Grunting looked at each other and shook their heads.

The moon and stars were soon covered up by clouds.

"Storm is coming," said the Siren as they all drifted off to sleep.

Chapter V

Humble Beginnings

In the middle of the lush green forest was an open meadow with an old farmhouse and a stable. The buildings were rickety and old but strong and had been there for a while. Captain Ruhk and Crystal sat at the breakfast table and argued about whether Crystal should learn how to fight.

"You need to defend yourself and I can teach you how to use the sword. I have years of experience to teach you so the same things that happened to me don't happen to you," said Captain Ruhk.

"You have to protect me. I need not learn the sword so long as you're with me. What we need to do is play hide and seek," said Crystal.

"Eventually you are going to want to go out on your own and I won't be around forever. What kind of a father would I be if I didn't prepare you for that?" Captain Ruhk asked her.

"A great one, because then we would have more time to play," said Crystal. Captain Ruhk let out a small sigh of frustration, pulling some fingers over his eyes to rub them.

"You promised me you would keep that necklace safe, are you going back on your promise?" he warned.

"No," she replied. Crystal grabbed her necklace and tried to hide it from her father. "Alright, so a quick lesson then play time, OK?" Crystal asked pleadingly.

"It's a deal," he said, excited that his daughter would finally learn how to use the sword. Captain Ruhk jumped up from the table, grabbed his sword and then quickly found another that was tarnished and partially burned.

Tiara awakened from her nap only to find Tarragon at the opening of the cave, deep in thought.

"Tiara, come," beckoned the deep-voice of the ancient dragon. Tiara walked cautiously over and sat down at the cave entrance next to him.

"Yes, sir," she said, her voice was soft and wary.

"You must not leave this cave until I release you. There are dangers in this world and I can't keep you protected from what is hunting you. I will teach you everything I have learned over these long years so that you may protect yourself," Tarragon stated.

Then he smirked and turned his head towards Tiara. "To start with, I will teach you reading and writing in both the common tongue and the magical language. I will teach you to use magic responsibly, including all of its aspects, from Conjuration to the forbidden Necromancy. These are dark times, child, and we must survive them by any means necessary. Do you understand?" asked Tarragon trying to be careful not to rant for too long.

"Yes, please teach me." Tiara looked up at Tarragon and the smirk on his face faded slightly as he realized all the basic things he must teach her first. "I suppose Arithmetic will also be necessary," Tarragon said.

Training began for Tarragon and Tiara in the dark, wet, and nearly sunless cave. As the months and years passed, Tiara's skin became as white as snow as she learned all she could from the dragon.

"The magic hand can be used to pick locks from across the room, or take the keys from a jailor, or to bring a weapon back to you, should you lose yours. *Bimanous Uida*," said Tarragon. And Tiara watched as a rusty old weapon flew up from the ground and soared towards him. "Now you try."

Tarragon continued to each teach Tiara different spells which included summoning a bright shining light, and conjuring a fireball only to launch it towards the cave wall. As promised, Tarragon also taught her the darker sides of magic and she regularly practiced summoning skeletons and ghouls, then destroyed them with her fireball spell. She also practiced using magical plate armor, which is clear save for the center of the armor, similar to the likes of the white center of an ice cube.

As Tiara's magical strength grew daily, Crystal was fast becoming a keen swordsman. Training daily in the beautiful, but hidden meadow next to the farmhouse, Crystal's skin was now light with a sun-kissed tan from training and playing out-side. Sparring with his daughter, Captain Ruhk called out the different sword movements. "1, 2, 3, 4, and 5. Very good. Now 6, 7, 8, and 9," he dodged to one side, slightly out of breath as Crystal put him through his paces. "I'm getting too old for this," he panted. "Yes, 10, 11, and 12, that's my girl!"

"This is getting too easy, pop!" cried Crystal.

"Yeah?"

"Show me what you've got, old man."

The taunt brought a smile to Captain Ruhk's lips. "If that's what you want." Turning, he ran into the farmhouse with Crystal close behind.

"What-?" But before she could finish, he attacked and the fight continued in earnest. They ran all throughout the house, knocking over the kitchen table, using chairs as shields, fighting in and out of doorways when someone knocked on the front door, causing Captain Ruhk to pause and look over at the door. Crystal quickly disarmed him but before she could revel in her victory he put a finger to his lips.

"What? Who is it?" she whispered, looking back and forth between her father and the door.

"You have been doing really well in your training, and have finally learned all I can teach you. So, I've planned a little graduation ceremony," he said with a smirk.

"Really?" Crystal said excitedly.

"More like a final test," Captain Ruhk said, correcting himself.

Captain Ruhk opened the door to a woman in her early to mid-30's dressed tarnished armor with white hair and carrying a ball-and-chain on her shoulder by a metal clip that hooked onto the handle, keeping it out of her way by letting the ball and chain free fall behind her.

"Crystal, meet Dame Eclipse. Madam, this is the trainee I was telling you about," Captain Ruhk said with a warm and welcoming smile.

"Pleasure to see you again, Captain Ruhk," she said, entering the house and holding out her hand. Captain Ruhk took her hand and kissed it like a gentleman.

"The pleasure is mine. This is an old acquaintance of mine," he said, turning to Crystal. "She joined the army at a very young age though she just helped with the paperwork back then," Captain Ruhk teased.

"That didn't stop you from teaching me how to fight," she add with a small smirk. "You must be Crystal. I'm Dame Eclipse. Your father tells me you're quite the swordsman," she said.

"Thank you, he's been training me for some time now, to prepare for the return of the future Queen," said Crystal.

"Your father also tells me that you've kept the Royal Pendent safe all these years," Dame Eclipse said, looking at her curiously.

"Pops has been keeping me safe so the credit should go to him," Crystal said softly.

"She's just being modest. I've never had to worry about the pendent even when she was young, she's always taken good care of it," Captain Ruhk boasted proudly.

"Now, I have a small test. I challenge you to a fight, first one to disarm the other wins," Dame Eclipse stated.

"I'll do my best," replied Crystal.

"Good, then let us begin. First, choose your weapon." Dame Eclipse unclipped the ball and chain from her shoulder.

"Now, Crystal, she has a ball-and-chain so remember-"

"Dad!" Crystal called out with frustration.

"Alright, sorry," he said, backing off.

Dame Eclipse smiled slightly and stood with her weapon ready. Her ball and chain had a wooden handle with an iron spike at the butt end, and was wrapped in a leather strap. The handle was about a foot long with an iron chain at the end that linked to a solid iron ball covered in metal spikes. Crystal picked up a long sword and held it against Eclipse's ball and chain, and then the battle started.

Dame Eclipse took an aggressive stance and swung her ball and chain in a small counter-clockwise motion. Then she took a swing at Crystal, pushing her back and knocking her off balance. Crystal took a few steps back, put both hands on her sword and moved to a defensive position. Eclipse swung at Crystal's head, forcing her to duck and roll out of the way. Quickly standing, Crystal then attacked, thrusting her sword forward. In reply, Eclipse swung her ball-and-chain forward, wrapping it around Crystal's sword. She stepped out of the way at the same time.

Their weapons were caught together; Dame Eclipse made a circular motion with her hand and yanked Crystals' sword out of her grip. The sword slipped from the chain and flew across the room. Crystal jumped for it and just caught it before it hit the ground. Eclipse walked over and swung whilst Crystal rolled onto her back. She parried the attack and then kicked

Eclipse back with a firm shove to the stomach. Making the most of the opportunity, Crystal jumped to her feet. Eclipse and Crystal both swung at each other, their weapons meeting in a clash that reverberated through the small farmhouse. They pushed back against each other, locked in a battle of strength. Sensing a checkmate, Crystal eased the pressure on her sword, letting Eclipse come forward for a split-second before pushing back with all her strength, throwing Eclipse off balance. Crystal then continued her attack as she freed her sword and swung again.

Eclipse fell down, off balance, and used the butt end of her ball-and-chain to parry Crystal's sword. Eclipse braced her free hand on the ground and caught herself. As she got back on her feet, Eclipse put her shoulder into Crystal, forcing Crystal back. Putting both hands back onto her ball and chain, she swung at Crystal's side. Unable to stop the attack fast enough, Crystal fell to the ground, the spiked ball only just missing her. Following the motion of her weapon, Eclipse swung at Crystal's sword arm, knocking it above her head with a sickening crunch. Crystal gave out in pain.

Crystal was on the ground, defenseless. Eclipse held her weapon above her head and stepped on Crystal's sword hand to disarm her. Crystal yelled out in pain as the heavy metal on Eclipse's boot crunched the bones in her hand. Using her free hand, Crystal hit the back of Eclipse's knee, taking the weight from underneath her and forcing her to fall to her knees. Without hesitation, Crystal wrapped her arms around Eclipse and rolled her onto her back. She quickly grabbed her sword and held it to Eclipse's throat.

Eclipse swung at Crystal's sword hand again but this time Crystal swung back, aiming for the weapon's wooden handle, and knocked it to the ground. She then used the blunt side of her sword to knock the inside of Eclipse's arm to loosen her grip on her weapon. Crystal then quickly kicked it out of her reach and Crystal smiled.

"Yeah baby!" shouted Captain Ruhk, almost jumping for joy

"I yield, you have beaten me," said Dame Eclipse.

Crystal helped Eclipse up and dusted her off. Dame Eclipse picked up her weapon and re-attached it to the clip on her shoulder. "Good job, it is not very often that someone beats me. Well, take a knee, if you don't mind," she said, slowly catching her breath. Crystal warily bent down and kneeled on one knee.

Dame Eclipse went outside and reappeared carrying a beautiful sword with an ivory handle and a shiny steel blade with ripples down both edges, almost like small waves.

"This is the sword of the first king of Abbigonia. Whilst it is not in my power to name you as a knight, I can, however, name you as captain," said Dame Eclipse.

"What?!" exclaimed Captain Ruhk in surprise. Dame Eclipse laughed.

"I'm just kidding," she said. "By the power vested in me," she said as she rested the sword on Crystal's left shoulder. "By my rank in the army of Abbigonia." She moved the sword over Crystal's head. "I dub you, Corporal Crystal." And finally tapped the sword on Crystal's right shoulder. "Rise Corporal Crystal. Take this sword and protect it, as you have protected the Royal Pendent all these years," Dame Eclipse said.

Crystal stood up and took the sword, her eyes welling up.

"I'm so proud of you Crystal, Eclipse where will you go?" asked Captain Ruhk.

"Captain Ruhk, I'm going to the Lost Harbor to meet Admiral Stevens of the Black Mast Pirates. It's a small port town near the edge of the kingdom. I'm going to offer them amnesty in exchange to join the resistance. If you need me, I'll be there," explained Dame Eclipse.

"What makes you think they will join us?" asked Captain Ruhk.

"Any loot they find as they attack, they will be able to keep. It was a pleasure to see you again, Captain. Corporal, congratulations," said Dame Eclipse.

Dame Eclipse walked out the door and hopped onto her horse, before riding off into the forest. Captain Ruhk and Corporal Crystal looked at each other as the white-haired knight rode off in her continued quest to fight for the old kingdom.

Chapter VI

Heroes!

Two people walked along the road and soon came upon a ragtag village that looked as if everything was a hundred years old. Most of the buildings could have easily been considered abandoned. The first person wore shining armor without a scratch on it. It was rubbed to a shine and beautiful. Metal clanked from head to toe as he walked and a long sword swung by his side. The other wore a red and purple robe and carried an old staff that looked like it might have been a tree branch that was trimmed to look like a staff.

"Remember, if they ask, I'm a knight. And what are you?" Chasten the Knight asked, glancing over at his friend in the robe.

"Spell-Luminator. It's a fancy term for a battle wizard," said Triskelon.

"Ok, wait, I have to sit for a minute," said Chasten as he found a suitable spot to rest.

"What's a battle wizard?" asked Triskelon.

"Someone who only took the time to learn the attack spells." Chasten rolled his eyes.

"Oh, right. I can see the town from here," said Triskelon, pointing further up the road. After Chasten felt rested, they continued walking until they were stopped by a few guards stationed on the road.

"Stop! You are entering the town of Krylon. Who are you and what business do you have here?" one of the guards asked in a loud, boisterous voice.

"We, my friend, are heroes! We have come here to test the limits of man-spell and steel," Chasten boasted boldly.

"Where is your leader? We need to speak with him," Triskelon said more calmly.

The two guards looked at each other for a second, slightly amused. "Go see the Mayor, he should be in the town square somewhere," said the second guard.

The two heroes walked into the town and made their way towards the center where a few men looked around and pointed at them as they talked. On officially looking man was stood in the middle directing and pointing, issuing orders.

As the two heroes neared, Triskelon turned to Chasten, "I guess these guys?"

"Yeah, probably. Mr. Mayor?" Chasten said once they were close enough.

Mayor Tomwell stopped his current conversation and noted the two strangers stood in the middle of his town. "Hello gentleman, what can I do for you?" he asked.

"I am Chasten, the Great Warrior of Abbigonia!" Chasten said pushing his chest out and putting his fists on either side of his hip.

"And I am Triskelon, the wondrous Spell-Luminator of Abbigonia!" Triskelon said raising his staff up in to the air and making a flash of light spring from its end.

"We are heroes, walking from town to town, helping the people in their time of need. Do you need anything done?" Chasten asked.

"There is a lot to do around here on any given day, but for heroes? How do I know you're not with the king?" Mayor Tomwell said half-jokingly with a raised eyebrow. The two heroes looked at each other and thought for a moment. Then Triskelon shrugged his shoulders.

"The Legendary warrior always sides with the people," Chasten stated.

"Always for the people!" Triskelon said almost as if an idea had just come to him.

One of the two people standing either side of the mayor suddenly whispered something into his ear. Then the other person whispered into his other ear. The Mayor raised his hand to call off his advisers. He looked them over and thought for a moment.

"I have just the job for two heroes such as yourselves," he finally said. "Fires around the town provide warmth for the people and it helps the guards to see at night," he said, pointing to a few different fires around the edges of the square. "Lately, we have been running out of firewood and need more to keep them going. We need you to go out and chop down a few trees for our stockpile," Mayor Tomwell ordered.

"Yes, sir! You can count on us!" Chasten and Triskelon spoke in unison.

"Good, there should be a few axes around the lumber pile somewhere. Go ahead and get started," Mayor Tomwell said, quickly dismissing them again and going back to his previous conversation.

The two heroes went over to the town wood pile and looked around, eventually finding two rusty axes. They picked them up and headed out into the forest.

The heroes picked out an enormous tree that would take many people a long time to cut. "This one looks good? I'll go first," Chasten said with a quick yawn and a stretch of his arms.

"Yeah, sure, this one is good. All we have to do is chop it down, boom. Wood pile is restocked," Triskelon said with a wave of his hand, as if to say it wasn't a problem.

"Yeah, this'll be down in no time," Chasten said gripping the axe tightly and taking careful aim at the tree. After 15 swings, Chasten placed the axe head on the ground and leaned on the wooden handle. He was breathing heavily and sweating profusely. "Ok, your turn," he panted.

"Are you kidding me? You haven't even gone through half the tree," Triskelon complained.

"We don't have to, after we chop a third of the way through, it should just fall over," Chasten said trying to convince his friend to help.

"Doesn't it have to be three quarters done?" Triskelon asked with a frown.

"No, with these big trees, the weight just pulls them down."

There was a sudden noise nearby and Triskelon jumped, turned and eyed the forest warily. A pair of red eyes peered out through the bushes. There was another sound and the eyes disappeared, only to reappear at another hidden spot.

"Did you see that?" Triskelon said in a panicked voice. The eyes disappeared.

"See what?" Chasten said, looking around. "Stop trying to get out of work." "Something moved those bushes back there," Triskelon said with his eyes now darting anxiously around.

"It's just your imagination. Go ahead and start chopping," Chasten ordered.

The red eyes peered at them again from the other side. Then the creature made a low growling sound from its spot in the bushes.

"There it is! Look!" Triskelon said looking to Chasten with a finger pointed at the bush.

"I see it?" Chasten said, no longer concerned with chopping the tree. "What do we do?"

"Run?" Triskelon said looking down the pathway that lead deeper in to the woods.

"We can't run, we're heroes! We have to at least see what it is," Chasten said.

"Alright, go get 'em," Triskelon said watching Chasten's reaction.

"No way, I'm not going in there," Chasten said, picking up his axe and gripping it tightly.

Just then, a wolf jumped out from the bushes behind them and growled loudly. He had pure white fur and red eyes, with sharp teeth the color of bone.

"Holy!" Triskelon shouted and began running down the forest pathway without looking.

"By the Gods," Chasten said, dropping his axe to follow Triskelon.

The two heroes ran deep into the woods. They strayed off the beaten path in a panic, soon finding themselves lost.

"I think he's gone," Triskelon said turning back to look.

"I'm surprised we just out ran a wolf," Chasten said, huffing.

"Where's the path? Where are we?" Triskelon asked noticing his surroundings.   The two looked around futilely, then looked at each other in understanding.

"Shall we make camp then?" Triskelon said trying not to say the obvious.

"Yeah, this is as good a place as any," Chasten said.

Finding a few twigs and logs nearby, they piled them up. Triskelon summoned a small fireball and shot it into the pile, which sent them everywhere.

"Darn it, pick them up quick, before the fire goes out!" Triskelon said, scrambling around picking up the smoking twigs.

"They're going out!" Chasten said, falling to the ground and doing the same.

Triskelon froze when he saw two familiar red eyes peering at him. Chasten paused and looked at him, confused.

"Hey, what's wrong with you? The fire's going out, we need to hurry!"

"W-w-w-wooo," Triskelon tried to speak but panic gripped him.

"What?" Chasten replied, half annoyed.

The wolf came out of the shadows and quietly sat down behind Chasten.

"Th-theere is a, is a woo," Triskelon tried to say again.

"I didn't know you stuttered this bad," Chasten said putting his twigs back into the pile. The wolf let out a loud, piercing howl causing Chasten to shriek in surprise, "A wolf!" He jumped next to Triskelon, both of them now facing the wolf as it slowly moved closer, a low growl coming from its throat. They edged back and found themselves up against a large tree.

"I, I tried telling you," said Triskelon.

"Maybe if you weren't tripping over yourself in fear, I could actually understand you," Chasten said.

"I didn't see you having trouble keeping up with me back there when we were running through the woods, with all that armor on" said Triskelon.

"Yeah, that staff isn't doing you much good right now either," Chasten said as they started to curl up. The wolf abruptly stopped its growling and sat down in front of them. He gazed at them with an almost lopsided grin.

"You two are hilarious," it said.

The two heroes looked at each other in shock and then back to the wolf.

"It talks," Chasten whispered.

"The name's Mistral. Shall we get this fire going? It's going to be cold soon."

"He has fur, how does he get cold?" Triskelon whispered back.

Mistral walked over and lay down by their pile of smoldering twigs.

"I don't think he wants to hurt us," whispered Chasten. "He could have done that already if he wanted to." Triskelon nodded and cautiously tried to re-light the fire. Mistral smiled as he heard that last comment.

"What brings you two out here, anyway?" Mistral asked the two supposed heroes with a small smile as he watched them struggle.

"We needed some wood to replenish the nearby town's stockpile," said Triskelon.

"That giant tree would have given you a lot of wood for sure."

"And we'd be finished by now if you hadn't chased us away," said Chasten.

Mistral laughed. "It would have taken you a month to chop it down at your rate."

"We're heroes so we handle this sort of thing all the time," Chasten boasted.

"Yeah, I suppose that's why you're chopping wood," Mistral said playfully.

"No, really, we are heroes!" Triskelon defended.

"Sure," replied Mistral.

There was a moment's silence.

"You don't have any food, do you?" Chasten asked.

"Let me just check my satchel for my rations" Mistral replied sarcastically.

Triskelon at him. "You have a satchel?"

Mistral looked at Triskelon in amazement. "No, I don't have a satchel," he scolded. "How on earth would I actually keep, put things in, or anything else, with a satchel?" Mistral sighed in frustration and turned away from them. Chasten and Triskelon looked at each other with a smirk.

"Yeah, stupid, what's wrong with you?" Chasten teased.

"Hey, you're the one that asked if he had food."

"True," Chasten admitted softly.

The two heroes eventually got the fire going and all three of them lay down next to it for the night. As they looked up toward the sky, a silence fell over the camp. The crackling of the fire and the random snapping of the logs were all that could be heard. The stars lit the way for dreams as they all drifted off to sleep.

Chapter VII

Not Enough Wood

I t was late at night and the cold night air filled the camp. Chasten woke up half frozen and found that there was nothing left of the fire except for a few hot embers. Looking around the camp, he saw Triskelon and Mistral huddled together for warmth and still asleep. Scanning the ground in the nearby woods for sticks he could throw on the fire, he found nothing.

"That's it, I'm freezing. I have to find more wood," he said as wearily stood up and started to trudge through the forest but it was to dark to see any spare wood on the ground. His eyes were half open as he looked to the ground for fallen wood. He trudged on and the ground started to lean upwards, causing him to struggle and push with each step forward. Realizing he hadn't been paying attention, nor had he found any firewood, Chasten stopped and looked around. He found that he was walking up a mountain and, looking up toward the sky at the stars, he saw a soft light illuminating the entrance to a cave.

"If that light is a fire, they might have some spare wood," he said to himself. "I hope it's not a troll., just a quick climb," He spat into his hands and rubbed them together.

Excited because he would be warm again, he started to climb higher. There was a second of silence as the wind blew past the cave before a hand reached up and braced itself on the earth, then another. Chasten's face appeared at the edge of the ledge in front of the cave looking ridiculously tired from climb. He lifted himself up to his waist and let out a long-winded breath of exhaustion.

"Oof." He flopped onto the ledge and took a moment to compose himself. As he caught his breath, he looked out from the ledge and could see the entire forest.

"Great view," he muttered as struggled to his feet. I made it. Oh, my god that was a mistake. Warmth is near." He took one step, then another and walked into the fire-lit cave.

"Hello? Is there anyone here? Can I share your fire?" Chasten asked slowly, starting to catch his breath and squinting to see into the poorly lit cave. He continued walking into the cave and saw a girl lying next to the fire, the most beautiful girl he had ever seen.

"Wow," he whispered to himself.

A few more steps forward and he was close enough that he could feel the warmth from the fire and so he stood with his hands held toward the flames as he stared at the girl. Then he saw the dragon that was deeper in the cave. He panicked and covered his mouth as he tried not to yell out.

Chasten turned around, starting to tiptoe out of the cave, but the sound of his metal boots on the cave floor suddenly seemed to make too much noise in this tight space.

Disturbed by the noise of Chasten's shoes, Tiara woke up, her eyes slowly drifting open as she yawned and stretched to see someone creeping around the cave.

"Tarragon, wake up! Assassins!" Tiara yelled as she jumped to her feet and summoned a gust of wind.

"No, I'm not... I didn't mean to, ooof-" Chasten was suddenly thrown onto his back by a strong gust of wind.

"Don't knock him off the cliff," Tarragon demanded as he quickly woke up and started to charge toward Chasten. As the giant beast stood over Chasten and breathed heavily, Chasten started to panicked.

"Please don't eat me; I don't even know who you guys are. I'm not a threat to you, I promise," Chasten whimpered.

"Who are you?" Tarragon boomed.

"Chasten. I'm Chasten, the legendary warrior of the..." said Chasten, as he trailed off incoherently, trembling on the ground.

Tarragon raised an eyebrow. "What are you doing up here on my mountain?" he asked.

"I saw the light from the fire and I was cold. I...I didn't know it was your mountain. It's a lot further to climb than it looks," Chasten said with a chuckle, trying to lighten the mood.

"You're an adventurer and you don't know how to make a fire?" scoffed Tiara. "Can you read and write?" she asked, not believing a word he said.

"You might be able to see well enough in the dark to start chopping wood, but we ran out of firewood and I couldn't see three feet in front of me," Chasten replied, defensively, desperately hoping he wouldn't get eaten.

"Who knows you're up here?" Tarragon asked, puffing smoke into his face to get his attention.

"No one, my friend's still asleep, by the fire, the one that's gone out. The fire we set last night but I woke up and was cold..." said Chasten.

"He jumped out and scared you?" Tarragon asked Tiara, barely listening now as Chasten began to babble.

"You're much scarier," muttered Chasten. "And she is really pretty. Can I stay by your fire?" he asked with an air of desperation in his voice.

"Go find your own cave, moron." Tiara pointed to the entrance, before walking back to where she'd been sleeping.

"Please, I'm freezing and not looking forward to that climb back down. I can offer you hardtack and water, but its back at my camp," Chasten said trying to bargain with what little he had. Tarragon considered his offer for a minute. "Please, you can tie me up, I don't care. My sword is back at the camp, too."

"Let him come in, put him in a cage next to the wall," Tarragon finally said.

Tiara stood up and started to cast a spell. Fire and smoke mixed in the air and slowly started to take shape. It formed a large cage with metal bars on all sides. Before it had fully formed, Tarragon carelessly grabbed Chasten and dropped him inside before curling back up to go to sleep.

"There. Stay there until morning, legendary warrior," Tiara mocked.

Chasten chuckled softly and watched Tiara as she lay down. Then he stretched his hand out towards the fire, relishing its warmth.

"No problem here and I know you won't forget me. Try as you might," said Chasten playfully.

"Well that's true," said Tiara, as she lay back down and fell asleep. Chasten stretched his hand out towards the fire.

"Oh, fire. I can feel you," Chasten whispered to himself.

"When you were making the fire, didn't you think, *Hey, maybe this much wood won't get us through the night?*" asked Tiara.

"Well there were a few other things on my mind at the time," Chasten said.

"Oh, sure, I guess you can only concentrate on one thing at a time," Tiara said sarcastically. Chasten laid down, stomach to the ground with his hands stretched out as close to the fire as he could reach and fell asleep.

Chapter VIII

Battle in the Cave

The next morning, Tarragon nudged Tiara with his nose. It was early morning, and the sun was just beginning to rise, its rays barely reaching into the cave.

"Tiara, wake up child," said Tarragon in a hushed voice.

"Mmm, what?" she asked still sleepy-eyed.

"It is time to leave," said Tarragon calmly and quietly.

"Really?" she asked, sleep suddenly forgotten. "What are we going to do with him? I guess we can't just leave him here to die."

Tarragon thought for a moment. "I suppose not. We either take him with us or release him and leave him here. He was able to climb up, he'll be able to climb down," Tarragon suggested.

"Think he will be good for anything?" she asked eyeing the hero suspiciously.

"I'm not sure, I guess that depends on how many friends he has close to the king," said Tarragon.

"If he is close to the king, we should keep him prisoner and get as much information from him as possible," said Tiara.

"Let's interrogate him and find out what he knows. He didn't seem like the sort last night," Tarragon admitted begrudgingly.

"Sounds like a plan," Tiara said softly.

Tarragon let loose a loud growl that reverberated, which was loud enough to wake up Triskelon and Mistral down the mountainside. Chasten woke up and immediately, pushing himself against the cave wall in panic.

Tiara quickly waved her hand around the cage, turning it back into smoke and then dropped to the ground as Tarragon shot a ball of fire against the wall of the cave right next to Chasten.

"Hey, don't eat me! Did you spare me last night to eat me this morning?" Chasten questioned panicking due to the way he was woken up.

"Do you have any connections with the King? Did the King send you here?" Tiara asked in a loud and commanding voice.

"No, I promise. I've never met the King," said Chasten.

"Oh, ok, he promises. I guess he's alright then. Blast him!" Tiara said.

Tarragon shot a fireball at the wall on Chasten's other side and he let out a shriek.

"No, don't blast him! Do I look like a barbarian to you?" Chasten said with his hands going over his armor as if to point it out to her.

"I think he's clean, a chicken, but he's not connected with the King," Tarragon said, and relaxed some.

"Who are you? And what are doing out in these woods? Don't you know it's dangerous for idiots like you?" Tiara asked accusingly.

"It might be dangerous for idiots maybe, but not for heroes!" Chasten said with a smile. He stood up tall, placed his fists on his waist and puffed out his chest as he looked out toward the clouds.

"Right," Tiara said with a roll of her eyes.

"Oh yeah," Chasten said as he looked at Tiara and winked.

"Whatever. I will only ask you this one last time before you become dragon food. What were you and your friends doing out in the woods?" Tiara asked as she summoned a fireball that hung suspended above her flat palm.

"Chopping wood for a nearby town, so they could keep up the local fires protecting the town. Do I have to become dragon food? Can you guys just take some of my hardtack or something?" Chasten asked, looking from one to the other.

Tarragon's growl had echoed through the trees and woken both Triskelon and Mistral in a panic. It only took them a moment to realize Chasten was missing.

"Chasten? Chasten!" Triskelon yelled out whilst searching between the trees. Mistral put his nose to the ground and started to search for Chasten's scent. Then he paused and sniffed again before letting loose a howl to get Triskelon's attention.

"We're coming buddy, hang on!" Triskelon yelled out as he followed Mistral further into the woods.

It wasn't long before Triskelon and Mistral came to the mountainside where Chasten had climbed up the night before.

"He's up there in that cave," Mistral said, pointing his nose towards the cave entrance.

"How did he get way up there in the middle of the night?" Triskelon asked with a chuckle.

"You have to try and fly us up there," Mistral said, looking back and forth between Triskelon and the cave entrance.

"Fly us up there? I'm a battle mage, not a gryphon" Triskelon said, trying to think.

"Well, float us up there then. Come on hero, think! Can you actually cast spells or not?" Mistral urged.

"Yes, yes, of course I can cast spells but I'm a battle mage," Triskelon said as an idea came to him. He started to wave his arms and cast a spell that created a tornado. The strong winds spun around them as the leaves and trees around them started to push in a single direction as the Maelstrom became more prominent. As it picked up strength, it lifted them from the ground and they started to spin around faster and faster. Eventually they moved further up to the top of the vortex and continued to spin round and round.

"I think I'm going to be sick," Triskelon said, covering his mouth with his hand as his face started to turn green.

"Mage, if I survive this, I'm going to kill you," Mistral shouted over the deafening sound of the winds the spinning was getting him sick as well.

The sounds of a tornado outside the cave interrupted Chasten's interrogation. They watched as a wolf and man in the centre of the whirlwind kept spinning before it launched them into the cave toward them.

"Look out!" Tarragon yelled. Tarragon and Tiara only just ducked out of the way as Mistral and Triskelon flew toward them. Mistral hit Chasten square in the chest and sent them both flying against the cave wall whilst Triskelon landed on the ground next to the fire in the middle of the cave. Quickly recovering, Tiara reached her hand toward the dying fire. "I call upon you mighty fire, aid me now," she said.

A stream of fire launched toward her and surrounded her as her veins turned to magma and her eyes a fiery red. Tiara turned her gaze toward Triskelon and summoned a fireball. Triskelon leaped up produced a small fire in the palm of his hand. A little dizzy from the maelstrom earlier. With the fire in one hand, Triskelon took his other hand and spread the fire into three small balls, throwing each at Tiara one after the other.

Tiara jumped out of the way, launching a fireball of her own. She hit Triskelon and sent him deeper into the cave, slightly singed from the fireball and out of breath from the smoke.

Mistral stepped forward and started to growl at Tiara, baring his teeth, his fur stood up on his back. Tiara took a breath and her skin and eyes turned back to normal but when she saw Mistral, she started to talk in another language. Her eyes turned white as she bent down and reached her hand out gently toward him, still talking in the strange language.   Mistral, shocked she could speak in the animal language, stopped growling and stared at her.

"Wolf, I am the daughter of the old King and Queen, I am not your enemy," said Tiara in the animal tongue.

Mistral slowly took a step forward.

Meanwhile deeper in the cave, Triskelon stood up and summoned a lightning bolt in his hand.

Chasten saw what his friend was doing then looked back to Tiara. He then looked back to Triskelon, then back to Mistral who was now being petted by Tiara and came to a conclusion.

Triskelon squeezed his hands together to concentrate the lightning bolt and as he launched it towards Tiara, Chasten ran and threw himself in front of it. The bolt launched both Chasten and Tiara into the air and they both landed with a heavy thud.

Tarragon charged toward Triskelon, releasing a long breath of fire down the cave. Black with smoke and coughing from the dragon's fire, Triskelon didn't see Tarragon's claw come hurtling through the darkness. Tarragon threw the battle mage up against the wall, knocking him unconscious.

Tiara struggled to her feet, pushing Chasten's heavy bulk off of her. She got ready to cast another spell, and took a second to look around to see Tarragon carrying Triskelon over in his mouth and drop him next to Chasten.

"Why did you do that? You stepped in front of his lightning bolt," Tiara said, trying to what make sense of what had just happened.

"Triskelon probably thought you'd kidnapped me or was going to eat me, or something! I don't think you would have done that," Chasten said with a shrug of his shoulders.

"I'm sorry I attacked you," said Mistral.

"Don't worry about it. You were reacting to what you saw," Tiara said, taking a deep breath.

"What happens now?"

"We should tie them up. We can bring them to the nearby town and see if their story is true," Tiara said, nodding to herself.

"Perhaps a little more information might lead our way as well. We should get to know the people in this area and try to get them on our side," Tarragon said, knowing that Tiara was almost ready to claim back her kingdom.

"A dragon swooping in and tossing down two tied up people who claimed to be heroes ...that shouldn't scare anyone at all," Chasten said playfully.

"Maybe if you chop down some of the trees they said they would and brought them the wood, that would give you a chance?" Mistral suggested.

"No, I have a spell for them. I'll make sure their fires will never run out again. No matter how much wood they have," Tiara said thinking quickly to one of the many spells she had learned from Tarragon over the years.

"Alright, just be careful. We don't want to start some sort of witch hysteria," Tarragon said cautiously.

"Right, we will," Tiara said confidently. Quickly summoning a long rope, Tiara tied up Triskelon first. Chasten held out his hands and let himself be tied up.

"Do you always like tying people up?" Chasten asked with flirty smirk.

"Do you always have a dirty mind?" Tiara said, yanking his rope a little tighter.

Picking up one end of the rope, Tiara enchanted it so that Triskelon and Chasten floated in the air. Dragging them along, she climbed on to Tarragon's back.

"Wolf, what is your name?" Tiara asked in the animal language.

"Mistral, the ancient wolf spirit. And yours?" Mistral replied looking up to Tiara.

"I'm Tiara, and this is Tarragon. Come, follow us, we need a good wolf like you," Tiara replied.

Mistral howled his reply.

Tarragon took off with the two heroes being dragged behind.

Mistral hesitated a moment, "After all these years they have finally come back. The stories were true?" Mistral asked to himself.

As Mistral then took off and followed them from the ground, he looked up. He had some difficulty as he slipped and surfed down the rocky mountain and then jumped to a running start. He followed them through the forest and laughed at Chasten and Triskelon as he saw the them hanging upside down from the magical rope that Tiara and Tarragon was clinging onto. Chasten and Triskelon waved to Mistral playfully as they saw him following them.

Chapter IX

Proof of Identity

Tiara, Tarragon, the two tied up heroes, and Mistral soon arrived at the nearby town. Mistral, looking up, followed the two heroes and almost ran into a town guard.

Tarragon flew in a circle around the town and decided it seemed safest to land in a small clearing near its edge. The two heroes dropped next to him as he landed and chaos ensued. The town's people screamed and ran from the dragon and the magical floating people. A town guard almost too scared to attack, froze in place. The two heroes looked at each other with a smile.

Tiara hopped down from Tarragon and walked toward the center of town.

"Who is the mayor of this town? We do not intend to harm you, we only seek answers to our questions," Tiara shouted loudly.

After a moment's silence, Mayor Tomwell nervously stepped out of the crowd. "I'm the Mayor of Krylon. You seek answers? What answers? What do you want?"

"Krylon? There is no town called Krylon that I remember," Tarragon said half to himself.

"How long have you slumbered, dragon? This town has only been recently established," Mayor Tomwell said with a slightly more self-assured tone about himself.

"These buildings look old though," Tarragon said suspiciously.

"Did you hire these two idiots, I mean heroes, to gather wood for your town? Or is that a fabrication?" Tiara pointed to the tied-up heroes and looked at Mayor Tomwell.

"Yes, I did. The town fires help the guards see at night and we need wood to maintain them," Mayor Tomwell confessed with a slight amount of amusement to himself.

"I think I can help you with that, if you'll let me. I can make it so you'll never have to cut wood again, and the fires will always burn," Tiara said gesturing to the surrounding town.

"Why are you helping us? Who are you?" Mayor Tomwell asked.

"I don't want to your money. Our people have suffered a lot in these past years and I have only recently returned to the kingdom. I intend to rectify that if I can. I only ask you one thing, do you love the King?" Tiara asked inquisitively at Mayor Tomwell, playing at a hunch she had.

Mayor Tomwell cleared his throat and thought about the old rumors that one day the true queen will return to the kingdom then answered her, "The people of this town have mixed emotions about our King. We let any barbarians in our town to avoid complications with the king. That is why there are so few of us," Mayor Tomwell defended with a strange amount of nervousness to his voice.

Tiara walked over to one of the town fires and uttered the necessary words, spread her arms out around it. "Proprius incendia," she whispered softly. The fire flickered violently for a second, then an orange haze surrounded it and eventually faded.

Tiara made different hand motions while she said the spell words but each time the spell fizzled out. She first tried a figure eight, but then it soon fizzled out. Then she tried to motion a number four, but that again fizzled out. Finally, she tried a sideways figure eight, and the spell took she spread the small blue fire from her hands to the town fire, which turned all the flames blue.

"Take a stick from this fire and put it in every town fire, and they will never run out. I give you my word on that. But in return I must ask that you don't tell the King about us, for something larger," Tiara said staring into the fire a moment.

"Do you realize what you're asking of me and my people?" Mayor Tomwell said in shock.

"Yes, I do. It's not a reasonable request. But I promise that I will bring you hope for a better future," Tiara said with a confident nod.

Mistral, sat next to the two heroes and gave a quick nod to say hello to them as he sat down spoke, "Tarragon, where are we headed next?"

"Tarragon? The King's dragon? He died in the final battle along with the King, the Queen, their daughter and Captain Ruhk. Everyone died," Mayor Tomwell said in confusion.

"Who told you this?" Tiara asked curiously, looking around at the townsfolk.

"It's been common knowledge for years. They all died." Mayor Tomwell said with a small frown.

"I didn't, and I will return. I am Tiara, daughter of the old kingdom. I'll say the things you wish you could, I'll do the things you've only dreamed. I'll bring hope to those who remember the old king. And I'll save those who are lost. I am Tiara, daughter of the old King and Queen, and the rightful heir to the throne of this kingdom. The dragon behind me is Tarragon. At the final battle we fled the town just before King Tentaclous' men stormed the city. Side with me in the upcoming conflict and I'll see to it that the King answers for all the injustices he's committed. I'll see to it he answers for his crimes and that he will face the peoples' justice," Tiara said confidently and firmly.

"And if we die in that battle?" Heckled someone from the crowd in a sarcastic tone.

"Then we died together fighting for something we all believe in. Know that you can say no, and continue to do what you have been doing, but the king will come, and his army with him. Eventually they will catch you and you will be forced to fight. Could you beat his army alone?" Tiara asked as she saw the fear flicker across the mayor's face.

"For years you have lived in fear avoiding the King's men. Side with us and together we will strike fear into the heart of the King himself. We will usher in an era of prosperity and freedom that this kingdom has longed for since its destruction," Tarragon said, sensing Mayor Tomwell's reluctance. But the crowd started to mutter in agreement.

"We haven't much choice, have we?" he replied. "Avoiding the King is one thing. If you're forming an army to fight back, then count us in. Anyone that stands against the King will need allies, and someone to coordinate it all; we will fight," Mayor Tomwell said tugging at his own clothing.

A cheer erupted from the townsfolk around them and Mayor Tomwell smiled proudly.

"We will fight," he repeated.

"We will return. Until then, prepare weapons and armor and start stocking up on food and water. When I return, war will be upon us," Tiara said, giving one last look around the town. She walked over to Tarragon, letting out a quiet sigh of relief, and then climbed back up onto his back, grabbing the rope attached to the two heroes and made them float in the air behind her again. Tiara whistled at Mistral for him to jump up behind her. With a flick of his tail, Mistral jumped up onto the dragons back as Tiara waved goodbye to the townsfolk.

Tarragon spread his wings, gave several powerful flaps of his wings and slowly began to lift off the ground. "Hang on," Tarragon yelled as he went higher over the tree line.

"I don't have any thumbs to hang on with," Mistral said, placing his head against Tiara's shoulder.

Mayor Tomwell watched them fly away before turning to his people, "Need allies, hah. That and an insane amount of luck. Send a messenger to the King; tell him that the daughter

of the old King has returned, and that she's amassing an army."
Mayor Tomwell said not giving Tiara another thought.

Chapter X

Weaseling her way In

The Siren, Mudmucker, Grunting, and Noctremis came upon an old ruin of a castle. The walls and guard towers crumbling, the remains only a shadow of what they once were. The town was nearly burned to the ground, and its people lived in the tumbled down structures, and however they could.

The Barbarians swarmed around the central castle and throne room. Droves of war-torn, half-rusted armor, and muscle-bound invaders maintained control over the people of the town.

Slowly, the four villains walked through the streets, receiving looks of disgust from the town's people along with looks of curiosity from the barbarians. Hushed whispers fell over the town as they made their way to the main entrance of the castle. One of the menageries of Barbarian guards began to speak as they walked up.

"What on earth are you four?" one of the Barbarian guards asked bluntly.

"Such beasts are not welcome in Barbarian lands," stated another.

"We are here to see the King; we have information about the old king's daughter. As the law has it, I am entitled to an audience. Now move or I'll curse this town's ale with frog's mouth," said the Siren, with Grunting, Noctremis, and the Mudmucker standing proudly behind her.

The Barbarian guards moved mostly out of the way and opened the doors to the castle. As the four villains walked into the castle, Noctremis pushed into the others nervously, trying to stay as close as possible. The doors closed quickly behind them, slamming loudly against the stone walls.

The four villains walked through the dark and decrepit hallway of the ruined castle decorated with an old torn rug on the wall and a torch that once lit the hallway now lying smoldering on the ground. Eerily, they walked down the hallway to a loud room where light could be seen spilling from the doorway. The doorway led to the old throne room where King Tentaclous sat on the throne surrounded by gold and silver objects. He drank and partied with his victorious army.

Boldly, the four villains walked halfway into the room and addressed the King. "Great and mighty King, I humbly seek an audience with you about the old King's daughter," the Siren said with a polite bow.

"You are a Siren that is clear. Why should I even bother listening to a witch such as you? Tell me why my minions shouldn't tear you apart right now," King Tentaclous said gesturing to some of his men.

The Siren formed a wide toothy grin. "We both know you are the greatest fighter in the world. That is why you are the Barbarian King. However, against an entire kingdom of people who believe the old King's daughter is greater than you, even as a child. To this day, she remains hidden, and you grope the kingdom searching for her still," the Siren said cunningly, playing the King.

"They have left this land, never to return! I have beaten these people into the very ground itself. No one will remove my crown," King Tentaclous shouted angrily.

"The old King's daughter and her dragon have returned. Look at these claw marks, too large for a lion or a tiger," the Mudmucker said and pointed to the scars on his body.

"He also got a good look at the face with the dragon's claw. They were in a cave on the side of a mountain not overly far from here," the Grunting teased.

The other barbarians in the room laughed and chuckled.

The Mudmucker turned and looked at the Grunting. He stuck out his snake like tongue at him.

"Silence, you fools. I'll handle this," the Siren snapped. "The cave was just beyond the forest."

King Tentaclous thought for a minute and looked over to a cracked window that overlooked an open field on a big hill. Then he looked back to the four villains.

"Captain Clod, have your men scour the kingdom. Find this cave they speak of. Also, look for non-barbarians organizing the gathering of weapons and armor, horses and such. The storm of war may be upon us. You four stay here and if I find lies in your claims, all of you will soon find a new separation between your shoulders and your head," King Tentaclous snarled at the four villains.

"There must be a great reward for information such as this. How many years has it been?" the Siren asked, already pushing for a reward.

"If we find the missing old King's daughter and the dragon, your riches will be endless," King Tentaclous said with a smirk.

"We could help your men prepare for them, we have the experience, but it would require you to allow us among your ranks," the Siren said, trying to manipulate the King.

The King paused for a moment, considering her suggestion. "Done. I will make you a ranking officer in my army. These three behind you will be under your command," King Tentaclous said with a quick gesture.

"Thank you, great and noble King," the Siren said with another bow. The Siren then let out an evil cackle that could be heard throughout the castle and around the ruined former capital.

Chapter XI

Together Again

Tiara, Mistral, the two heroes, and Tarragon flew just above the forest. Mistral sat up front with his mouth open and tongue out whilst Tiara sat behind him and searched through the trees below.

"What are we looking for again? It all looks the same to me," Tiara said as she narrowed her eyes.

"A farmhouse, or an old cottage, or a hut in the middle of a small clearing or a meadow," Tarragon said, also scanning the tree line.

"Did you stash a cache of weapons inside it before the kingdom fell or something?" Tiara asked.

"No, we will get proof you're the daughter of the old King," Tarragon explained.

"Proof, what kind of proof?" Tiara asked.

"Your father, the old King, knew that if they fled, King Tentaclous would never stop searching for them, which would endanger you. And if King Tentaclous found you, the necklace of our people would be doomed to his rule. However, by staying and standing up to King Tentaclous, it motivated our people and created the legend of the necklace and the true Queen to remind the people not to give up. And King Tentaclous didn't believe the King and Queen had sent away their only child."

Tiara stopped searching the trees and looked down at Tarragon.

"So, King Tentaclous didn't come looking for us?" Tiara asked herself half under her own breath.

"Nor did he search for the missing necklace. As soon as he took over, he continued his march to other kingdoms. But when he left, the people started to rise up, one after another all over the kingdom. His army stayed in our kingdom and have continued to fight for dominance ever since."

"But what about now? Is he looking for us now?"

"Here are a few buildings," Tarragon said, suddenly changing course and beginning to circle above an open meadow with an old farmhouse and stables. Tiara leaned to one side for a better look. As Tarragon circled around the farm house, she saw two people hard at work, one tending to the plants and vegetables while the other took care of some horses.

"This one fits the description. There are two people down there," Tiara said with a pointed finger. As they got closer, Tiara saw the one tending to the horses suddenly pull them back inside and call to the other. Looking up from the vegetables, the second figure looked older. Running out into the middle of the meadow, she could make out it was a man who was now waving his arms back and forth over his head.

Crystal saw the giant dragon-shaped shadow on the ground then she looked up and jumped back, her jaw dropping as panic set in. She saw a dragon with a rider and a wolf and two people tied up, that circled around their farm house. "Father! Dragon!" Crystal yelled as she quickly pulled the horses back into the stables. Captain Ruhk looked over at Crystal, and then as she yelled, he looked up and squinted as his eyes at the flying beast. Suddenly Captain Ruhk smiled and waved his hands back and forth wildly. He jogged across the yard to where he could be seen easier. "That's them! Hang on, I'm going to land," Tarragon said, while giving his wings a few flaps to land softly and properly land on the ground. Mistral and the wolf looked around himself questioningly as if to say, "hang on to what?"

"Got it," Tiara said, placing one hand on Tarragon's scales and the other around Mistral as Tarragon picked an opening in the meadow and slowly lowered himself to the ground. His wings slowed and stretched as his feet touched the ground and he let out a sigh of relief once he'd landed. Tiara and Mistral hopped down off of Tarragon's back and watched as the man approached them with a warm smile.

"Tarragon, old friend, it's been ages! How are you?" he said.

"I am well, but I do not bring good tidings," Tarragon said softly.

"That's like the last time we met," he said with a small chuckle.

"However, there is someone I want you to meet. This is Tiara, daughter of the throne," Tarragon said, nodding his giant head toward Tiara.

"It's a pleasure, Tiara," He placed his right hand over his heart and took a small and quick bow. "I'm Captain Ruhk. I served under your parents and look forward to serving under you." Captain Ruhk said in a gruff but distinguished way.

During these introductions, the second person Tiara had seen from the sky approached and she was surprised to see it was a young girl about the same age as her.

The girl waved, and said, "Howdy."

"Crystal, show a little respect. Tiara is your future queen."

Crystal smiled; she'd been waiting for this moment a long time.

"We don't know that for sure yet. Don't move, I'll be right back," Crystal said, and then ran into the farmhouse before anyone could say anything.

There was a silence before Tiara eventually said, "I'm pleased to meet you, Captain Ruhk. And I'm glad to see the loyalty to the old King and Queen lives on."

"Of course," said Captain Ruhk firmly.

A series of loud crashing sounds coming from inside the farmhouse interrupted their conversation. Captain Ruhk shook his head with a small smile.

"Well, this is fun," Triskelon said playfully, and then Triskelon and Chasten both chuckled.

"Why don't you come on in, make yourselves at home," Captain Ruhk said with a chuckle and a gesture to follow him.

"Thank you. What is it she's looking for?" Tiara asked warily as the sounds of more crashing echoed across the meadow.

"Tarragon, none of our doors are big enough for you," Captain Ruhk said over his shoulder.

"Of course," Tarragon said and then began talking to himself as he tried to remember the appropriate spell.

Tiara laughed. *"Homo forma parvus,"* she said with a smile to him as she walked inside.

"Ah, yes, *homo forma parvus*," Tarragon said as he cast the spell. He then began to shrink in size. His shape began to morph into that of a human with wings and scales all over his body. He stood up onto his two legs and started to follow Tiara into the house. Crystal paused a moment glancing out the window and gulped, looking faster now.

"Hey, whoa, don't leave us out here," Chasten and Triskelon said in tandem with each other.

"I guess it wouldn't hurt to have you come inside for a while." Tarragon waved his hand and the two heroes fell with a thump onto the ground

"Can you two walk?" Tarragon asked, not wanting to untie them.

"Sure, OK. Trisk. I'll step with my right, you step with your right," Chasten said. They both tried to take a step but almost tripped.

"Ok, you step with your left and I'll step with *my* left," Triskelon said.

"Sure," Chasten said, looking down at his feet.

Mistral and Tarragon looked at each other then they both looked back to the heroes. The two heroes tried to take another step and tripped again.

Tarragon laughed.

"The guy in front steps with his left and the guy in back steps with his right. It's not that hard, you idiots," said Mistral.

"That was the next version we were going to try. Right, Trisk?" Chasten said playfully.

"Yeah, that's right. Trial by error. Let's go," Triskelon said, backing up Chasten.

The two started to walk and eventually made it inside. Tarragon and Mistral walked in after them, shaking their heads and closing the door behind them.

Chapter XII

The Princess's Return

Inside the warm and cozy farm house, Captain Ruhk, Tiara, and Tarragon, all sat down at a large oak table talking whilst Mistral watched the two heroes argue with each other. It wasn't long before Crystal reappeared from another room clutching a pendant in her hand.

"Found it!" she announced as she walked over to Tiara and held the necklace in front of her.

"What is it?" asked Tiara.

"Grab a hold of it," Crystal said as her eyes drifted toward the diamond at the bottom of the necklace. Tiara looked at Crystal questioningly then slowly reached forward.

"Is this the royal pendent?" Tiara asked, a little disappointed; it looked a too mundane to be a royal necklace. She took hold of the diamond jewel for a few moments but nothing happened. A silence fell over the room as everyone watched. "Is something supposed to happen?" Tiara asked with a raised eyebrow.

"It's supposed to turn red if you're the heir to the throne" Crystal said in a half accusing manner, reluctant to release her hold on the pendant's chain.

"Well, necklace or no necklace, I'm going to avenge my parents and restore order to the kingdom, a color-changing pendent isn't going to stop me," Tiara said, defending herself.

Crystal looked at Tiara and then looked back at the necklace before finally letting go of the chain. Suddenly, the clear diamond started to turn ruby red and Crystal's eyes lit up with excitement.

"It's turning red!" Captain Ruhk said with relief.

Everyone looked on in amazement, Chasten and Triskelon included.

Crystal hugged Tiara excitedly and ran off into the other room, leaving a baffled Tiara still clutching the royal necklace who quickly slipped it over her neck.

"Crystal, what are you doing?" Captain Ruhk shouted after her.

"Looking for my sword so we can get this show on the road!" Crystal yelled back.

Chasten and Triskelon started to laugh quietly as they stood near the doorway still tied up.

Captain Ruhk rummaged in a nearby cabinet and took out a bottle of sparkling wine. He looked around, quickly counted everyone and took out as many glasses.

"Who wants a celebratory drink?" Captain Ruhk asked, already holding a glass for everyone.

"I'll just have a little." Tarragon said softly with a raised finger.

"I'll try some" Tiara said softly.

"This does call for a celebration. I'll have some, if you don't mind," Chasten said with a smile.

"You don't get any," Tiara said looking back to Chasten.

"But you're the true queen, we are with you," Triskelon said with a nod.

Crystal walked back into the room and spread out a map of the kingdom on the oak table, placing random things on each corner to keep it from rolling back up.

"So, do we stick together and try to rally the people, or should we split up to cover more ground more quickly?" Crystal asked the room.

Captain Ruhk, preoccupied with handing everyone a glass and pouring the wine, didn't answer. Tiara walked over to the table as she politely took a glass and looked over the map with Crystal. Captain Ruhk then walked over to Tarragon and whispered "Ourselves will mingle with society and play the humble host." Captain Ruhk and Tarragon both let out a loud laughter. .

"The Lost Harbor is here." Captain Ruhk pointed on a far edge of the map where a small tear had been made next to the sea. "That is where Dame Eclipse was heading. Plus, I have a few friends that are still around, Tarragon and I could go visit them. Some will be easier to convince than others. Tarragon, who was that guy in Ridgemont?"

"Oh yeah, erm, Hard...? Hard-something?" Tarragon suggested.

"Hardloff, Duke Hardloff of Ridgemont. He has the most experienced veterans in the land. We'll try him first," Captain Ruhk said.

"Is he still in command?" Tarragon asked thinking back to how long ago it was when he last saw him.

"Last I heard, he was. That was a few months ago," Captain Ruhk said scratching his chin.

"What is this town?" Tiara asked as she pointed to a gold spot on the map.

"That's the city of Grand Amour. It's supposed to be the most beautiful place. I've always wanted to go there" Crystal said in a not too subtle hint to her father.

"Well, we'll just have to make that our first stop then," Tiara said with a smirk.

"Really!?" Crystal asked giddy with excitement.

"Lame," Triskelon said in a half-jealous kind of way.

"Hey, quiet you. Don't be rude, at least introduce yourselves," Crystal said playfully to Chasten and Triskelon.

"No manners at all," Tiara said not even being bothered to look at them.

Crystal smiled and laughed.

Chasten and Triskelon side eyed each other and then shrugged.

"I'm Chasten, Legendary warrior of Abbigonia."

"I'm Triskelon, the Legendary Spell-luminator of Abbigonia." Saying proudly

"Your reputation precedes you," Crystal said with a smirk.

"If Chasten the love-puppy hadn't stepped in the way of my fire ball, this situation might be a little different," Triskelon said defending himself.

"Maybe; maybe not," Crystal said with a shrug of her shoulders.

"Love-puppy? Love at first sight doesn't exist," Tiara said matter-of-factly.

"Better a fool in love than a fool with a sword and shield," Chasten said slightly upset that Tiara wouldn't even look at him. Crystal bumped Tiara playfully.

"We're going to the city of love, huh?" Crystal said playfully with a giggle.

"Don't listen to them. They'll say anything to get out of their bonds," Tiara said coldly.

"Are you going to do anything?" Tarragon whispered to Ruhk.

"She can handle herself," Ruhk responded.

"Listen, if we wanted to get out of these bonds we would, it wouldn't be that hard, honestly," Triskelon said with a nod.

Tiara turned and looked at them both. "Do it then," she said with a hand on her hip, waiting and watching.

"Alright, gladly." Triskelon nodded to Chasten. The two heroes struggled, pulling and twisting but did not untie each other.

"Easy, is it?" mocked Tiara. Crystal giggled.

They continued to struggle to no avail and eventually Triskelon gave up, quickly summoning a fireball to destroy the rope with fire.

"Fire!" Chasten yelled out as the ropes burnt off them and fell to the wooden floor, where Chasten and Triskelon stomped out the flames.

Triskelon awkwardly chuckled as everyone turned around and looked to where the fire was at. After seeing everything was fine, Mistral, Tarragon and Captain Ruhk looked back at the map and continued to discuss what to do and where to go.

"No problem," Triskelon said with a smile.

"And that's just a small show of our power," Chasten said with a flex of his arm muscles.

"Well, you guys did get out," Tiara admitted. "I stand corrected."

"Yeah, if you guys are the greatest hero's maybe we shouldn't start an uprising. We won't need to," Crystal said, eyeing them both playfully.

"We don't even need to start one; us two can take on the whole barbarian army by ourselves," Chasten said with a serious look followed by a loud chuckle. Tiara and Crystal laughed, one of them placed a hand over their stomach and the other placed a hand on the other's shoulder.

Realizing the others were currently planning out a strategy, they turned back to the map.

"If we march here, we would have a direct route to the castle," Captain Ruhk said.

"Yes, but we meet here; otherwise we'd have an extra day on our hands," Tarragon said pointing to another spot on the map.

"What's the point in going to the Lost Harbor? Could we just skip that all together and just move in?" Mistral asked curiously.

"If King Tentaclous is getting reinforcements from another port somewhere, then it's vital we cut off that resource," Captain Ruhk explained.

"And if Dame Eclipse was successful in gathering a small navy that is one less thing we need worry about," added Crystal.

"A navy built of pirates and swashbuckling scallywags is hardly something I think we should rely on," Tiara said dismissively.

Chasten and Triskelon approached the table and looked over the two girls' shoulders at the map. Tiara and Crystal turned their heads wearily then looked back to the map, deciding it was ok.

"Beggars can't be choosers. Besides, most of these people were once part of the Royal Navy, switching to piracy after the takeover," Captain Ruhk said with a confident nod.

"But there will be pirates there, real pirates that is, seeing as how it's probably now a heaven for pirates and outlaws alike," Tarragon warned.

"Which places have an official army we could use?" Tiara asked slightly overwhelmed by the amount of land they would need to cover.

"Grand Amour, Ridgemont, the Lost Harbor, and Meadowvale," Crystal answered, pointing to each location in turn; every major city in the kingdom besides the capital.

"What's in Meadowvale?" Mistral asked.

"A contingent of knights," answered Captain Ruhk.

"And what's in Grand Amour?" Tiara asked next, following them on the map listing them all in her head one by one.

"Archers, they're famous for their archers. The ones we're trying to get. They have some foot soldiers as well."

"Their foot soldiers are well trained and there's a lot of them. It would be wise to try to enlist them too," Tarragon said.

"What about Ridgemont? Is there even anything left?" Crystal asked, knowing they had recently attacked it.

"Experienced foot soldiers who love to fight. Led by an old war dog that's a friend of mine," Captain Ruhk replied.

"It only went under siege a month ago. There's probably nothing left by now," Crystal replied.

"Duke Hardloff was a good friend, now we're moving it would be great to get him on our side, and knowing that other people are moving within the kingdom may give them the edge they need to push back," Captain Ruhk said hoping she was wrong.

"So, Ruhk, you and me are to go to Ridgemont, then?" asked Tarragon. Captain Ruhk nodded.

"Crystal and I will go to Grand Amour, then" Tiara said.

"Okay, and then Tarragon and I will go to the Lost Harbor and try to find Dame Eclipse," Captain Ruhk said.

"Tiara and I can then go to Meadowvale," Crystal said moving her finger from one location to the next on the map.

"Hey, what about me?" Mistral asked with a whine, afraid they had forgotten him.

"And us?" Chasten said.

"Oh and we forgot about Krylon," Tiara said pointing to an empty spot in the forest.

"Krylon?" Crystal asked unaware of that town.

"That sounds like a Barbarian name," Captain Ruhk said narrowing his eyes.

"He didn't look like one," Tiara said quietly, a knot forming in her stomach. Captain Ruhk looked at Tarragon for acknowledgement.

"I have no idea about Barbarian names or anything like that. He looked human but it's been a long time since I've seen any," Tarragon said with a shrug of his shoulders.

"Where was he?" Captain Ruhk asked.

"His small town is about here," Tiara said circling a portion of the map with her finger.

"That's in the middle of the forest," Crystal said and then looked at Tiara doubtfully.

"Ok, how about Crystal and I go to Grand Amour then go meet in Krylon. Mistral and the two wonder idiots can go to Meadowvale and get the knights," Tiara suggested, briefly pointing to Chasten and Triskelon.

"I'm not comfortable with this," said Captain Ruhk eyeing Chasten and Triskelon carefully. "First, they're tied up as prisoners, and now you want to trust them to rally the forces?"

Chasten elbowed Triskelon.

"No, it's cool, we can handle it. And Mistral can show us the way," Chasten said, looking at Mistral with a thumbs up and a smile.

"We were only prisoners because we attacked you, well, them. But we didn't really know who you were," Triskelon tried to explain.

"I'd buy that, anyone stupid enough to attack Tarragon has got to have no idea who they are," Mistral laughed.

"Ye-" Chasten started then paused to scowl at Mistral. "Plus I wouldn't try to anger the most beautiful girls in the whole kingdom," Chasten said with a sweet smile to Crystal and Tiara.

"Aww," Crystal said, placing a hand over her heart.

"Yeah, well, know that if you fail or betray us, you'll be begging to go and join Tentaclous and his army, understand?" Tiara warned pointing her finger at each of them. Chasten and Triskelon took a gulp and then glanced at each other.

"Yes ma'am," Chasten tried to say as sincerely as possible.

"Alright, well, when you meet with Mayor Tomwell, don't move. In fact when everyone gets their army, let's meet up in Krylon and stay put," Captain Ruhk said sternly.

"Sounds fair enough. Mistral, you know the way?" Triskelon asked.

Mistral stood up on his back legs and put his paws on the table. He took a quick look at the map, then hopped back down and walked over to the heroes.

"Yeah, I know the way, it's pretty easy from here," Mistral said.

"I'll take the map," Crystal said as she started to roll it up.

"Let's pack up and get ready to go. Not sure if we'll have enough time to set off today," Tarragon said as he glanced out the window to see the position of the sun in the sky.

"We need to leave, light or dark. Time is running out and we need to get our forces together," Tiara said as she started to get ready to head out.

"My queen, I understand you want to end your people's suffering and take your rightful place, but traveling in the dark, running into the wrong person. The king put a price on your head large enough for all of us to live very happily for the rest of our lives and our next 3 generations as well. We should wait until morning," Captain Ruhk reasoned carefully.

"We need to be realistic here, and smart. One night isn't going to make or break anything," Tarragon added.

Tiara paused. "Ok, then let's start preparing."

"Crystal do you want to gather up some food, I'll go prep the horses," said Captain Ruhk.

"Don't condemn me to the kitchen," Crystal complained.

"Well, what do you want to do?" Captain Ruhk asked with a sigh.

"Prepare the horses?" Crystal asked with a smile.

"Alright, go get the horses ready. Tarragon, want some more Champagne? You three," he said pointing to Triskelon, Chasten and Mistral, "down in the cellar there's some preserving salt and some canned goods go. I need you to start bringing it all up here," he said, pointing to the cellar door. The three nodded and left the room.

"Come on, I'll show you the horses," Crystal said as she grabbed Tiara's hand and ran outside.

Captain Ruhk grabbed the bottle of Champagne and walked back over to Tarragon. "Well, old friend, it looks like the day has finally come," Captain Ruhk said as he sat down next to Tarragon.

"Yes, it seems as though it has. I've been dreading this day for a long time," Tarragon replied.

"Don't worry, she has us at her back," Captain Ruhk said reassuringly with a friendly pat on the shoulder. Time started to drift as the old friends caught up.

Chapter XIII

Preparing the Food

Chasten and Triskelon walked down the steps into the dark and musty cellar. The ground was soft with dirt and water mixed together. The wooden walls were partially rotted and dirt was beginning to fall out from between the planks that made up the walls. Shelves lined one wall and were stacked with loosely placed papers. A barrel full of salt sat in a semi-clean, dry area of the cellar floor. More shelves held labeled cans of food.

Chasten and Triskelon looked around the cellar curiously reading the different can labels and briefly shuffling through some of the papers. Chasten looked up to the cellar door to make sure it was closed.

"So, what do you think about the black-haired one?" Chasten asked mischievously as he looked at Triskelon.

"I think she's annoying. Not really my type," Triskelon said dismissively, continuing to look around the room.

"Yeah right. Come on, you were diggin' on her. I can tell," Chasten teased, bumping Triskelon's shoulder with a playful punch.

"She has a cute laugh, alright?" Triskelon said with a smirk.

"I knew it, you're in luuurve," Chasten teased.

"I am not!"

"Yes you are, you're head over heels."

"No, you are. I just said she was cute."

"Ah-ha!" said Chasten triumphantly, pointing at Triskelon. "You said she had a cute laugh, not that she *was* cute."

"Will you shut up?"

"Just admit it."

"No."

"Yes."

"No."

"Yes."

"How are we going to get this upstairs?" asked Triskelon, pointing to the barrel and hoping to distract Chasten.

"Alright, do you think we need all the salt in this barrel?" Chasten asked as the barrel came up to his chest and was filled to the brim with salt.

"Yeah, wow. I don't see anything else we could put salt in it so I guess we have to take this" Triskelon said with a shrug to his shoulders.

"I guess just grab it from the top?" Chasten said with a shrug of his shoulders. Triskelon watched as Chasten tried to grab hold of the barrel a few different ways.   "That is never going to work."

"Well, it's going to need both of us." With a sigh, Triskelon went to help.

They each took a side and, grabbing the barrel from the top, tried to lift it, only managing to get it about an inch off the ground. The two grunted and groaned as they shuffled towards the cellar steps.

"You're going to fast," grunted Chasten.

"No, I'm not-"

They both tripped, spilling over half of the barrel onto the ground.

"Ooooh cripes!" yelled Chasten as he bent down and started to scoop the salt back into the barrel.

"Oh, by the gods. Quick, put it back in!" Triskelon panicked and started to do the same. "Don't let too much hit the dirt!" he whispered, glancing up the stairs to make sure the door was still closed.

After a while they stopped scooping the salt and stood the barrel back up.

"Well, you think anyone will really notice?" Chasten asked, scratching his head.

"Nah, but at least it'll be lighter," Triskelon said.

The two lifted the barrel of salt again and moved towards the stairs.

"Maybe I should go first, no armor on, you know," Triskelon suggested.

"Yeah, good idea," Chasten said. They rearranged their positioning and with a grunt, once again lifted the barrel.

They only managed 4 steps before Triskelon tripped and spilled more salt.

"Put it back in, on the double" Triskelon said as he scooped the salt back up into the barrel.

"We are going to be in so much trouble," Chasten said.

The two started up again and finally made it up the stairs. They continued into the kitchen where Tarragon and Captain Ruhk were sat at the table, talking and laughing.

"Gentleman, we heard a little noise down in the cellar. You happen to know what that was?" Tarragon asked, hiding his coy smile.

"The salt does look a little low," Captain Ruhk added with a quick glance at the barrel.

"No idea," Chasten said with a smile."It's just as we found it," he said and tapped the top of the salt barrel with his hand.

"We'll just go back down and get the cans," Triskelon said, quickly changing the subject.

"Yeah, be right back."

Chasten and Triskelon continued to go up and down the stairs to get the cans whilst Tarragon and Captain Ruhk enjoyed watching the two younger men work.

Chapter XIV

Gossip by the Horses

Outside the farmhouse, at the nearby stable Tiara and Crystal prepared the horses. There were only 4 stalls in the stables, each one filled with hay.

"This one differs from the others." Tiara said.

"That's a Mustang" Crystal replied, watching Tiara's reaction as she patted the horses.

"Are all Mustangs smaller?" Tiara asked as the horse warmed to Tiara quickly.

"Yeah, smaller than the Clydesdale's. The others are war horses, the Mustang. She was Pops' choice," Crystal explained as she prepared the horses.

"A good choice," Tiara said as she scratched and patted the horse with both hands, making funny faces as she did so.

"These are the war horses," Crystal said, gesturing to the other three stalls. "They can carry a knight wearing armor faster and longer than a Mustang could." Crystal tried to explain in a polite but bluntly matter-of-fact way.

"Can I borrow one?" Tiara asked.

"Of course, that was the plan. Now that Pops is going with Tarragon, you'll need a new ride," Crystal said, leaning against the gate of the stall where Tiara was at and smiled.

"So, do you like him?" Crystal asked, a playful smile pulling at her lips.

"Who? The Mustang? I've never seen one this color before," Tiara said not taking her eyes away from the horse. Crystal didn't reply and Tiara paused and raised an eyebrow. "What?"

Crystal covered her mouth and giggled. "I meant Chasten. He likes you, you know," she said still smiling staring.

"Maybe, I'm not 100% sure he's one of us," Tiara replied, quickly turning back to the horse with a small frown. "When the King Tentaclous hears about what we're trying to do, he's bound to put a price on my head. Who's to say those two idiots won't go for the instant gratification. You know?" Tiara said with a sigh.

"I didn't sense that. The one with armor seems to be sincere. Both of them are funny as well," Crystal replied.

"Yeah? You did seem pretty into Triskelon," Tiara said with a casual shrug of her shoulders and then covertly glanced at Crystal out the corner of her eye.

Crystal laughed. "No, nothing, I didn't felt nothing there." Crystal said denying the fact that she kind of liked Triskelon.

Tiara smirked and turned to lean against the stable entrance with her arms folded.

"Sure," she said, still smirking.

"Honest!" laughed Crystal.

"Well, I think they're both idiots. If it was my choice, I'd choose the Mustang," she said as the horse took a step forward in the stall and started to sniff Tiara.

"I'd suggest this one over here," said Crystal, skipping over to another stall and putting her arms around one of the Clydesdale's. "He's the most trained."

"But I want the Mustang."

"He's not really battle ready, he's barely even trained. In fact, he's as stubborn as a blasted mule. This one over here is our finest," Crystal said with growing frustration.

"That's OK. I can barely ride a horse, anyway."

Crystal gently took her hand. "All the more reason for you to ride a horse that knows how to act when it's carrying someone as important as you. Trust me, this guy's great," Crystal said showing off her prized Clydesdale to Tiara.

Tiara eyed the horse, unconvinced, and then looked longingly back to the Mustang.

Crystal sighed, placed her hands on her hips and narrowed her eyes at Tiara.

"You know, on second thought, I'd say you too are perfect for each other."

Tiara smiled. "Well, who else would take her? Your dad is going with Tarragon and he's the most experienced rider, probably, unless you wanted to take her. You could probably handle her fine."

"I'm not taking that stubborn thing. And if you're not taking him, I am," Crystal said, pointing to the prized Clydesdale.

"That's fine, you should take the finest for yourself anyway, and it's your horse. Plus, I don't want to hold up those two idiots any more than I have to," Tiara said playfully but with a hint of seriousness and respect in her voice.

"They seem capable enough as far as errand boys go," Crystal said with a shrug.

"You're joking, right? Chasten crawled up half a mountain to our cave just for a bit of warmth from our fire. His potential is downwards not up," Tiara said bluntly with a hint of inner rage erupting.

"At least he's persistent," Crystal teased sensing her inner rage.

"Those knights are important, maybe we should just keep them with us and go to Meadowvale together, after we've been to Grand Amour, and then meet up you're your dad and Tarragon," Tiara said thinking aloud.

"I'm sure they're not that useless. You said one of them climbed up to your cave? Then what, did you fight?"

"Yeah, maybe." Tiara said not knowing where Crystal was going with this.

"And he's still standing?" Crystal laughed. "So he must be able to take a hit. Maybe they could just challenge one to a duel and try to outlast him." Crystal playfully bumped her hip into Tiara's.

"Yeah, maybe they should. I would feel better knowing they couldn't screw it up." She sighed. "So, what do we need to do to prepare the horses?" Tiara asked distracting herself.

"Saddle them up, brush them down, that sort of thing. You shouldn't worry. The talking wolf will go with them. He has to know the forest well. And he can convince the knights to at least follow him. We'll just have to make sure we arrive at the meeting place before they do," Crystal said as she gathered up the saddle blankets and a couple of the saddles from the tack room.

"I suppose your right. I think we'll have our own problems, anyway. From what Tarragon's told me, the people of Grand Amour have never been very trusting. That could make it difficult for us." Tiara picked up the remaining two saddles.

"As soon as they see the necklace, they'll be on our side. We just need to make sure we don't run into any bounty hunters or mercenaries. They'll be looking for a ruby necklace," Crystal said while looking at the ruby pendant the reflection of the ruby in her eyes as she gazed at It hanging from Tiara's neck.

The two started to saddle up the horses, and Crystal brought Tiara through the steps.

"Step 1, groom the horse thoroughly."

"Step 2, place a blanket on the horses back, being sure to cover the withers."

"Step 3, place the right-hand stirrup of the saddle over the saddle horn and girth over the seat of the saddle."

"Step 4, stand on the left-hand side of the horse and hoist the saddle onto the horse's back. Now, make sure the saddle horn is right on top of the horse's withers and the saddle should lie evenly on the saddle blanket."

"Step 5, release the stirrup from the saddle horn and pull the girth down off the seat."

"Step 6, Sling the birth under the horse's belly just behind its front legs."

"Step 7, feed the cinch strap through the ring of the girth, and then back up and repeat it once."

"Step 8, Pull the strap to the left of the upper ring, and then cross over to the right."

"Step 9, feed the strap behind the upper ring and then through the ring to the front, tucking it under where it crossed itself."

"Step 10, Take up the slack in the cinch strap, pulling it from the bottom to fit the saddle snugly on the horse. Then you are done. Wanna try that other one?"

It wasn't long before they saddle all four horses up and ready to go. Crystal added more hay to their feed bins and then they headed back into the farmhouse.

"Everything ready?" Captain Ruhk asked as they walked in.

"Yup," Crystal answered with a nod.

"Do a final pack check before bed, once we leave that's it" Ruhk ordered knowing it was getting late.

It's almost dusk. We should get a good night's sleep tonight. It may be a few nights before we get a chance again," Tarragon said before standing up and heading off to take the spare bedroom.

"Right then, Tiara you'll have to share Crystal's room. You two can sleep in my study tonight," Captain Ruhk said, pointing to Chasten and Triskelon.

"You can count on us," Chasten said confidently.

"I'll get you some blankets and pillows. Tarragon, Mistral make yourselves at home. We'll head out at first light." Captain Ruhk said yawning. After that everyone started to head up to their room or make themselves comfortable. Ruhk made sure everyone was comfortable and then headed to his room for a good night's sleep.

Chapter XV

Betrayal

The doors to the throne room broke open and slammed against the castle walls. A messenger ran through the doors and up to where King Tentaclous and Captain Clod stood around a table in the middle of the room with a map on it.

"We have a group here, here and here," King Tentaclous pointing to different points on the map. "Then the royal one of course, here," he said as he pointed to the capital city.

"My Lord! I'm here with a message from Mayor Tomwell" panted the messenger.

"Spit it out then," King Tentaclous snarled.

"A girl claiming to be the daughter of the old king and queen is running amuck in your kingdom. She just came to our town trying to recruit soldiers for a rebellion!" he said in between gasping for air.

King Tentaclous froze. The messenger and Captain Clod anxiously waited for his reaction.

"Guard, release the Siren and her cronies and bring them to me," he said. Then he motioned for the messenger to come toward him. "Where is Mayor Tomwell's town?"

Said King Tentaclous a new fire burning within him now. The messenger hesitantly pointed to the map.

"There is no town there, what are you trying to pull?" Captain Clod said, glaring menacingly at the messenger.

"I must discuss this secret town with Mayor Tomwell later. For now, we need to find out where she's head to next," King Tentaclous said, looking down at the map and trying to think things through.

"She said she would return. After she gathers more troops" said the messenger.

King Tentaclous thought for a moment, looking at the different towns and cities on the map. Then he looked at Ridgemont and remembered he'd recently sent troops to attack the town.

The Siren and her cronies entered the room under armed guard, interrupting his thoughts.

"It turns out your information was correct, Siren. Where was she when you saw her?" King Tentaclous asked and gave an evil look toward the Siren watching every flick of her finger. The Siren walked up to the map and pointed to a mountain near the edge of the kingdom.

"Here, my Lord," she said.

"You said you saw her in a cave?" King Tentaclous asked.

"Might be why we never found her," muttered Captain Clod with a scratch to his greasy beard.

"Either way, she currently presents a serious threat. If she is aware of what's happening in the kingdom then she might know that I've recently sent troops to destroy the rebellion in the city of Ridgemont." He placed his hands on both edges of the map and could feel the frustration beginning to build.

"She, herself, is not a danger yet, my Lord. Only with her people behind her will she be a credible threat to you. Send everything after her and take her while she is weak then publically end her as a warning to all who oppose you," said the Siren.

"I say let her gather her troops and gather your own while she does so. Then fight her while she is at her greatest and you are at your greatest. It will end all future rebellions and the battle will be immortalized for all eternity!" Captain Clod suggested with a clenched fist he slammed on the table, filled with battle lust.

"My Lord, she is younger than you, and her troops have been suffering for half a lifetime under your rule. End her rebellion now before it becomes more than we can handle," the Siren protested.

"Enough both of you. Siren, you and your cronies go here, here and here. I want you to get the troops I've positioned there. There is a rebellion in Ridgemont, if the princess is there don't engage, if she isn't put an end to the uprising. Captain, go with the messenger and take your army to this hidden town. If the princess returns, bring back proof." King Tentaclous ordered giving Clod his second, the real orders.

"Yes, master. Messenger, you heard him," Captain Clod said, thwacking the messenger on the back of the head at the same time.

The messenger nodded and rubbed the spot where he'd been hit before hurrying from the room with Captain Clod close behind.

"Siren, if the battle is over bring the troops back here."

"As you wish, sire," she said as she gave a gracious bow and then left, her three cronies in tow.

Only King Tentaclous was left in the room.

"If that dragon is still alive, we will need a way to tear him out of the sky," he muttered. He looked at the map as if for inspiration. "I will crush the old king's daughter with my bare hands around her throat, if I have to. This kingdom is mine," he said with a confident and triumphant smile.

Chapter XVI

Fond Farewells

Captain Ruhk and Crystal were in the process of packing the horses. Tarragon lay stretched in his original dragon with a pack of food strapped onto his back. Chasten and Triskelon were going in and out of the house carrying the necessary items out to the horses. Tiara was reading a spell book, memorizing spells for the day.

"Crystal, you make sure all the straps are tight?" Captain Ruhk asked.

"Yeah, what's with the Mustang's saddle?" she asked, struggling to fix it.

"The buckle has rusted so you might just have to tie it."

"Done," Crystal said, finally giving up and just tying it.

"Who's getting the Mustang?" Captain Ruhk asked as he looked over the horses and there packs.

"Tiara."

"Does she ride well?"

Captain Ruhk asked inquisitively, knowing she probably grew up in a cave. "Maybe on a dragon."

Captain Ruhk chuckled.

"It's not funny, Pops. I tried to tell her."

"I'm sure she'll be fine, and with you to teach her."

"That's what I'm worried about," she muttered.

Once everything had been packed, the group gathered in a circle.

"Everyone know where they're going?" Captain Ruhk asked, looking around the group.

"I think so" Crystal said with an anxious smile. "We have the map, anyway."

"I've memorized the way to Meadowvale, so we should be good," Mistral said with a flick of his tail.

"You memorized the way?" Chasten asked, unsure whether he should trust the wolf's map reading abilities.

"Maybe we should give you guys the map," Crystal said looking to Mistral with a teasing smile.

"No, that's OK, ladies, you take it," Triskelon said.

"It's pretty easy," Mistral said, offended by Chasten's lack of confidence. "A straight shot there and back." He pointed with his nose to the direction they would be heading.

Tiara and Crystal looked at each other then looked back to the guys.

"All right, Tarragon are you ready?" Captain Ruhk asked with a new sense of seriousness.

"To Ridgemont!" Tarragon declared with vigor, crouching down as if he was about to take off.

"Yeah, all right, give us a hug then, Crystal. Tiara, you too," Captain Ruhk said before quickly embracing them one at a time. Then Captain Ruhk walked over to Tarragon and climbed up onto his back.

"OK, nice and slow at first, please, it's been a while," Captain Ruhk said with a few affectionate pats.

Tarragon stretched his wings out with a yawn and then began to beat them up and down. Slowly, Tarragon's body lifted off the ground. And with each powerful beat of his wings, they went up and up. They soared straight past the top of the trees then circled around the house and waved before flying off into the distance.

Crystal, Chasten and Triskelon all mounted their horses whilst Tiara struggled. Just as she'd gone to mount the Mustang, he took a step to the side, causing Tiara to stumble.

"He will be a pain in the butt," Crystal said, holding back a smile.

"If he keeps giving you trouble, just run him until he's tired," Chasten said.

"Since when were you a horse expert?" Said Crystal, twisting in her saddle to look at Chasten.

Ignoring them, Tiara started to pet the Mustang. She scratched his neck and whispered in his ear.

"What's she saying?" Triskelon asked as he knew it was magical in nature.

"I can't hear her," Chasten said, leaning forward to try to listen. Tiara abruptly stopped whispering and gazed at the horse for a moment. To everyone's surprise the Mustang took a step forward to help Tiara climb into the saddle.

Shocked, the four of them started to head out.

"Wow, talk about horse whisperer," said Chasten.

Mistral followed close behind, and muttered, "I can't believe that worked."

"There's a fork in the road up ahead. You guys should head off to the left," Crystal said waving her hand in the general direction.

"Sure," Chasten replied.

The four of them headed down the road; Mistral, Chasten and Triskelon in front and Crystal and Tiara behind them. Tiara slowly started to lean to one side.

"Tiara, are you sliding down?" Crystal asked, giving Tiara's saddle a questioning look. Tiara looked down at herself and at the horse.

"Am I?" Tiara asked unsure as she started to notice it herself as well.

"Take my hand," Crystal said reaching out toward Tiara. Tiara's horse reached a slight drop off in the road, which caused her to bounce in the saddle and inadvertently kick the horse. The kick made the Mustang think she wanted to gallop, he broke into a run. It zoomed off down the path as Tiara's saddle slid further. Unable to hold her balance any longer, she wrapped her arms around the neck of the horse and had only a single leg on the back of the horse, it had its neck straight out in an all out charge past Chasten, Triskelon and Mistral.

"Whoa, easy boy," Chasten said as Tiara ran passed him, desperately clinging on with only an arm and leg on top of the horse.

"Hey, wait, what the, ahhh!" Triskelon's horse, spurred on by the Mustang, took off after them. Unprepared for the sudden burst of speed, Triskelon tumbled backwards off the horse.

Tiara, unable to hold on any longer, took a leap of faith off of the Mustang's neck and fell to the ground. The horse kept running and slowly came to a stop. Chasten quickly rode up to Tiara, as Crystal caught up with Triskelon. Who had the wind knocked out of him.

"Are you all right?" Crystal asked as she reached down to help him up.

"Yeah, I'm fine."

"What happened there?" asked Chasten as he pulled Tiara to her feet.

"I have no idea. Are you all right Triskelon?" Tiara asked as Triskelon slowly stood up.

"That was quite a fall you had," Crystal said.

"Yeah, fine," Triskelon croaked as he gasped for air dusted himself off and tried to make it look like he wasn't in any pain. "No problem" Triskelon said in a strained voice.

Crystal rode over and gathered up both horses. Dismounting her own horse, she inspected the Mustang's saddle.

"Oops, it looks like the strap was a little loose on the saddle. Sorry, my bad," Crystal said.

"I think I just lost two years of my life from fear," Tiara said, taking a few deep breaths and then a chuckle.

"Even so, you'll still outlive these two, guys you should only live to about 25," Mistral said with a soft chuckle under his breath.

They all laugh and get on their respective horses. They continued to ride and talk together. Eventually they came up to the fork in the road. They gave each other a hug and went their separate ways. Tiara and Crystal went down the old road toward Grand Amour and Triskelon Chasten and Mistral went toward Meadowvale.

Chapter XVII

Battle of Ridgemont

Tarragon and Captain Ruhk arrived at a mostly destroyed city. Smoke and ruin covered all but the city's heart. The center of the city was laden with refugees, the local military trained to help defend the city and the wounded being tended to by doctors and nurses. Barbarians covered the ruins of the city and looked for any weakness to exploit as they continued to storm the defenses of Ridgemont.

"Stand at the ready brothers and sisters, we will strike fear into those barbarians yet!" Duke Hardloff shouted from the inner ring of Ridgemont's last defenders.

"Look, they're still alive!" Captain Ruhk shouted as Tarragon continued to circle around the survivors.

"Barbarians are on the charge," Tarragon replied, nodding to where there was an onslaught of attackers. They prepared themselves for battle.

Tarragon turned and started to sweep around the outer defenses of Ridgemont. He took a deep breath and breathed a ring of fire, temporarily stopping the barbarian attack.

"There he is, there's the Duke!" Captain Ruhk shouted.

"Ruhk, old boy," Duke Hardloff shouted, looking to the skies. "What a site for sore eyes! Listen, all of our people are here with us. Set the rest of the city a blaze."

"We'll give you time to regroup," Captain Ruhk shouted back. Duke Hardloff raised an arm in recognition before turning back to his men, after seeing the barbarians charge once more.

Tarragon took another deep breath and let out a large burst of fire from his mouth as he dodged spears, arrows and boulders that were being thrown at them from the ground. With Tarragon's fire burning through the remaining buildings and keeping the barbarians at bay, Tarragon and Captain Ruhk flew back over to the city's heart to find a small landing spot. Once they were back on solid ground, Duke Hardloff approached them.

"It's great to see you," he said, sheathing his sword. "I thought you died at the castle when Tentaclous took over."

"It's a long story and we are short on time, those fires won't last long," Captain Ruhk said looking around to see the fires were already starting to calm down.

"The king's daughter has returned. She's old enough to rule the kingdom and on the move. Will you stand with us?" Tarragon asked.

"We have already started a rebellion. But we can hardly help anyone right now," Duke Hardloff said gesturing to the troops and civilians around him.

"One battle at a time. Do you know who their leader is? Or where they've made their base camp?" Captain Ruhk asked.

"They have catapults in the east. That is where their base of operations is. My scouts report that there are more barbarians on their way." Duke Hardloff stated and pointed to where the balls of fire had been coming from.

"We could evacuate now, while the city is burning," Tarragon suggested quickly.

"That would take too long, and if they caught up to us, we would have to fight them on the move," Duke Hardloff replied. "We need a plan to attack the catapults and burn the enemy base camp. When they're leaderless, they won't have anyone to coordinate them and, considering how many they have lost already, they will retreat." He looked around, noticing the fires were slowly getting smaller and smaller.

"Right, we need everyone to maintain our borders so the civilians don't get hurt. Tarragon, fly high and out in front of us. Keep those fires burning, give us cover. Hardloff and I will charge behind your, fires and make sure their leader falls," Captain Ruhk commanded, unsheathing his sword and looking to the east.

"We may be able to turn around the incoming barbarians too. I'll cast a spell that will turn the spent weaponry against them, and protect the people," Tarragon said.

"That would require a substantial amount of magic. Are you able to do that and live?" asked Duke Hardloff.

"I may be old but I'm not dead yet," Tarragon said with a chuckle.

"Incoming! To arms!" shouted a soldier, interrupting their conversation.

"Hardloff, you ready?" Captain Ruhk asked as the troops prepared themselves for one last charge.

Tarragon leaped into the air, beating his wings. The force of his wings stirred the air, causing a small storm of dust and ash. Flames shot from Tarragon's mouth as he formed an easterly path of fresh fire.

"Stay clear of the catapults!" Tarragon yelled.

Duke Hardloff looked at Captain Ruhk as if to say I'm ready. "How did you convince me of this? I'm not as young as I used to be, you know," he said, shaking his head with a smile.

"Me neither, but it sure is a whole lot of fun."

The Duke chuckled.

"I guess it's true, you can take the dog out of a fight but you can't take the fight out of a dog," Captain Ruhk said with a laugh before charging with a loud and boisterous yell.

Hardloff and Ruhk ran behind the pathway of flames created by Tarragon. Barbarians closed in on them from both sides. They worked together and synchronized their movements to keep each other alive.

Reaching the catapults, they paused in shock as the wooden structures burst into flames. The barbarian's camp just behind the catapults was already on fire as well and Ruhk looked up to see the eerie silhouette of Tarragon disappear behind the clouds.

They ran into the camp and into the largest tent. A large barbarian wielding a large axe looked at them and then charged. Without hesitating, Captain Ruhk rushed at him, Duke Hardloff close behind. Captain Ruhk yelled as he met the barbarian leader in battle, the clash of his sword against the barbarian's axe reverberating around the tent. The barbarian leader was strong; however Hardloff and Ruhk were faster. As the barbarian swung wildly at Ruhk, forcing him to dodge and roll out of the way, Hardloff attacked on his exposed side. They attacked quickly and continued to dodge the barbarian leader's swings, one dodging the blow whilst the other attacked the barbarian's weaknesses. Exhausted from the onslaught, the barbarian was getting slower and slower until Ruhk and Hardloff attacked in tandem with one final blow, ending the barbarian leader.

Beheading the barbarian, Captain Ruhk carried the head out of the tent and held it aloft, yelling in triumph. Stunned, the nearby barbarians didn't move. Suddenly coming to their senses, they attacked all at once.

Readying himself for the onslaught, a wall of fire appeared between Captain Ruhk and the barbarians. Looking up, Ruhk saw the circling figure of Tarragon as he swooped in with another torrent of flames.

With no leader, no catapults and a fearsome dragon after them, the barbarians turned and ran.

Avoiding the retreating barbarians, Ruhk, Hardloff and Tarragon made it back to the city with ease, all of them breathing hard and feeling spent.

As they reemerged into the city' heart, there were cheers and celebrations from those still alive.

Tarragon paused and turned to the city gates. *"Libero Loricatus Telum,"* he said, blue and yellow wind pouring from his mouth. It sought the fallen armor and weapons, causing them to glow bright silver and rise from the ground. "Protect this city and its inhabitants at all costs," Tarragon commanded. In response, the armor and weapons began to patrol the streets of the city, chasing stray barbarians from within its walls. "It is done," Tarragon breathed, collapsing to the ground, exhausted.

"We will tend our wounded and finish training the volunteers for the city's new defense. The rest of the army is yours to command, Captain Ruhk," Duke Hardloff said with a grateful smile and a new sense of calm.

"Have you got a map?" asked Captain Ruhk.

Duke Hardloff called over one of his Captains who pulled a map from his belt.

"Meet us here in a few days' time. There is a small forest town not on the maps. Once there, we'll discuss what we're going to do next. Meanwhile, Tarragon and I are going to the Lost Harbor to try to catch up with Dame Eclipse."

"It's good she's still alive," Duke Hardloff said, still studying the map. "She will be a great asset."

"Hopefully, the navy is still in relatively one piece, one way or another," Captain Ruhk said with a shrug of his shoulders.

"This war might be useless if we don't cut off their lifeline," Duke Hardloff replied.

"Agreed. My daughter and the queen went to Grand Amour."

"I will hurry ahead a few scouts to make sure everything is OK."

"Thank you, I would appreciate that. Tarragon, do you need time to rest?" Captain Ruhk asked looking at the sprawled out dragon. "No, I'll be all right," he said, slowly getting to his feet. "I'll be ready to leave in the next few minutes."

"All right then, Duke Hardloff, until next time," Captain Ruhk said with a nod, holding out his hand.

"See you soon." The Duke clasped Captain Ruhk's forearm in a strong grip. They shook once and then broke away. Hardloff was unsure whether Eclipse and Ruhk would survive the lost harbor.

Duke Hardloff turned around and gave orders.

The refugees started to pick up their things if they had any. They walked back into the ruined city. Everyone eventually started to clean up and rebuild all over the city. "I'm ready," Tarragon said, giving his body one last stretching.

"To the Lost Harbor, then," Captain Ruhk said as he climbed up onto Tarragon's back. Tarragon jumped into the air, taking off quickly with a few beats of his powerful wings. Captain Ruhk looked back down at the Duke and yelled as they took off into the sunset. "Woooo hoooo!" Captain Ruhk yelled out as they zoomed toward the Lost Harbor. Duke stood waving, wondering if he'd ever see him again. Hardloff turned around and laughed to himself and shook his head back and forth.

Chapter XVIII

Gaining Trust

Crystal and Tiara rode toward the beautiful city of Grand Amour which was surrounded by a tall, granite wall. Two archers stood at the city entrance dressed in copper-plated armor with silver outlines at the edges. Crystal and Tiara approached the town slowly as the guards pulled out an arrow and made ready.

"What business do you have in the city of Grand Amour?" one of the archers asked, slowly drawing back his bow.

"I am Princess Tiara. This is my personal escort. Revolution is the business we have. Here is my proof," Tiara said confidently as she held up the royal necklace around her neck.

"Count Aldéric will determine the truth of your words," the other archer said as he lowered his bow and beat on the large gate with his hand. As it slowly opened, more guards appeared.

"Take her to see Count Aldéric," commanded the first archer.

Tiara and Crystal were escorted through the marble streets streaked with gold. Both the girls marveled at the city around them and the marble buildings streaked with silver. Even the benches and trash cans were made of marble streaked with emerald green. Like children on Christmas morning, they pointed out everything they saw.

As the procession made its way through the city, the citizens began to gather in the streets. They whispered to each other and pointed at the two girls on the horses, many more noticed the necklace Tiara wore and started to follow them.

"Can we stop there?" Crystal asked, spotting a jewelry store.

"Maybe on our way out," Tiara muttered, conscious of the people watching them and her necklace. Crystal gave a quick and playful pout but didn't say anything.

Eventually they came to the capital building. Tying their horses to the trough, they walked inside and taken to the study where Count Aldéric and his wife Charlotte were.

"What is going on?" Count Aldéric asked.

Charlotte set down the book she was reading and looked out her balcony.

"I don't know, maybe they are planning on storming the castle, worried about the wolf attacks" Count Aldéric said sarcastically. The butler walked in and cleared this throat. "Sir, two travelers to see you," said the butler.

"Travelers?" Count Aldéric asked, suddenly forgetting the mountain of papers on his desk.

Tiara and Crystal smiled and nodded. "Greetings, I am Princess Tiara and this is Corporal Crystal," Tiara said with a courteous bow.

"A pleasure to meet you," Crystal said with a smile and a wave.

"Princess?" Count Aldéric said with a scratch to his head.

"Where are you from, exactly?" Charlotte asked next.

"This is the royal necklace," Tiara said, avoiding the question.

"Can I see it?" Charlotte asked as she stood up quickly and walked over to Tiara, staring at the necklace.

"You wouldn't know what to look for," Count Aldéric snapped as he walked up behind Charlotte and playfully pushed her out of the way.

"I know more about diamonds and jewelry than you do, you big oaf," Charlotte mumbled gently nudging the Count out the way with her hip. She bent down to inspect the ruby.

"Ah, hush up, you old cow," Count Aldéric said playfully, holding the ruby between his forefinger and thumb, turning it this way and that and watching the light glint off it and holding it different lengths away from his eyes to see.

"Don't you tell me to hush up or I'll turn you into a dog again," Charlotte said, pointing her finger.

Tiara and Crystal just looked at each other in shock, unsure whether they could laugh.

Finally, Count Aldéric took out a pair of glasses but Charlotte ripped them from his hand before he could even put them on.

"Let me see those," Charlotte said as she put them on and focused on the ruby.

"You turn me in to a dog again, missy, and I'll... I'll..." Count Aldéric paused as he tried to come up with something.

"You'll what? Pat your leg while I scratch your neck?" Charlotte teased and then giggled. "Besides, I believe this is quite real."

"Are you sure?" Count Aldéric said, squinting at the ruby.

"I'm positive, it's real," Charlotte said excitedly.

"It's true then. My queen, it is a pleasure. However, my people might be harder to convince."

"I'll do whatever it takes," Tiara said.

"Really?" asked Charlotte.

Count Aldéric and Charlotte looked at each other.

"Perhaps a little test of your abilities, then? If we renew the people's faith then we can safely give you aid." Count Aldéric said

"How?" Tiara asked with a raised eyebrow.

"You're asking our queen to do a test?" Crystal asked in disbelief.

"It's just the matter of a wolf; I'm sure you can handle it," Charlotte said as she handed them a bounty paper.

"You expect me to put all our hopes into a stranger, into this... Joan of Arc, this teenager? If she is who she says she is, how would she have been raised? If she comes back with the wolf, we will know for sure she is who she says she is," Count Aldéric said sternly.

"Who is this wolf? Where can we find him?" Crystal asked, wanting to get on with things.

"Well, she's actually a werewolf. And lives out by an apple orchard not far from here," Charlotte said pointing to the bounty paper.

"We have seen it running back into the nearby woods to the west. The woods around there are all well covered except for the apple orchard. It's the only area in the forest where you can see the moon from the ground yet be close enough to attack the town every night," Count Aldéric said.

"Be careful, though, it's a full moon tonight," Charlotte warned.

"I see how our luck is going," Crystal sighed.

Tiara read the bounty paper and then asked, "Where is the orchard?"

"Follow the east road out of town and into the woods, just go straight ahead and it will open up to it," Charlotte said before she went back to her book.

"All right, we'll be back," Crystal said, happy to be leaving.

"And we'll be bringing the wolf with us," Tiara said, giving each of them a look before leaving with Crystal.

"Good luck," Count Aldéric shouted at their retreating backs thinking they will never see her again.

Tiara and Crystal walked out of the building and hopped on their horses. Then they headed out and rode toward the road as the sun set.

Chapter XIX

Moonlight Scare

I t was night, and the moon had shone through the trees. The shadowy canopy created a sense of unease that sent shivers down their spines. Crystal and Tiara hey slowly rode down the silent and eerie pathway. Both girls were on edge and jumpy. Tiara quickly turned around after every sound she heard in the forest.

"What was that!?" Crystal asked, startled by a rustling sound to their right.

"I don't know, I can't see a darn thing," Tiara said. "Oh, why don't I create a light?" she asked, half-closing one eye as she tried to remember the correct words.

"Nah, save your magic. Besides, the light might bring the wolf to us," Crystal said tightening her grip on the reigns.

Tiara's mustang suddenly stopped and munched at something within reach.

"Come on, let's move," Tiara said, giving the horse a soft kick to get him moving again, but he didn't budge.

"What's going on?" Crystal asked, holding back a smile. She rode over to Tiara and discovered the mustang was eating from an apple tree with low branches. "Oh, we must have come into the orchard without realizing it." Without warning, Crystal's horse started to eat apples from the tree as well, yanking the reigns from her hands.

"So, we're here then? Let's just walk, leave these guys to get their fill," Tiara said, climbing down from her horse.

Crystal looked down to her horse and giggled before dismounting. "Yeah, that horse can be stubborn from time to time. They'll be better protected from the wolf here anyway," she agreed.

Crystal and Tiara walked through the knee-length grass in the unkempt orchard, creating a pathway as they proceeded. They'd barely gone five steps when in between two trees they saw a young girl sat alone with her legs folded against her chest, her arms wrapped around her legs. She was wearing simple clothing that looked as tattered as if she'd been living out in the woods for a while.

"A girl?" Tiara said.

"We've got to get her out of here, before the wolf shows up," Crystal said running forward.

The girl gazed toward the sky when, after a moment, she began to shake profusely.

Crystal stopped in her tracks.

"Hey, you shouldn't be out here!" Tiara said, running to catch up with Crystal.

"She's shivering, she must be freezing," Crystal said looking to her clothes and watching her shake. Crystal moved closer and crouched slowly with a warm smile. "Hey, are you all right?" she asked softly.

But the girl didn't respond, she didn't even flinch or acknowledge that Tiara and Crystal were there. Instead, the girl continued to gaze up into the sky as if mesmerized. She suddenly started to shake more vigorously.

"Should we lift her up and carry her out of here?" Crystal asked.

"Maybe we should leave her, I have a bad feeling," Tiara said. The two stood and looked down at the girl for a moment. Crystal put a hand on her chin to help her think. Tiara looked up to where the girl was gazing as the full moon arrived and started to shine brightly in the sky. She looked back down at the girl and then back up at the moon. Tiara's eyes widened quickly as she jumped back and looked to the girl again.

"What?" Crystal asked startled.

"She's the werewolf!" Tiara cried out as she readied a few spells to protect herself.

The girl's breathing suddenly became heavier, and she panted. Her teeth grew longer and sharper, she grew in size and hair began to appear all over her body. Her eyes turned a solid white as her hands and feet turned into claws.

Now fully transformed, the werewolf jumped to her feet and gave out a loud and beckoning howl. Crystal grabbed the hilt of her sword and unsheathed it, jumping back to face the werewolf. Tiara took a couple of steps back and waved her arms around as she starting muttering. A translucent armor appeared, covering her head, chest, and legs.

"She's the werewolf," Crystal shouted in surprise.

"She's a criminal, knock her out," Tiara said circling around behind the werewolf. Without warning, the werewolf charged toward Crystal, its hands slashing the air in front of her. Crystal quickly took a few steps back, only just dodging the swings.

Dodging a few more blows, Crystal looked for the right opening to strike.

Tiara stood with her hands in front of her and started to circle them around an invisible ball.

"*Aeolus*," she said as the force between her hands began to build. The power of the ball was now so compact that fluctuations of wind could be seen between her hands. She struggled to contain the spell and turned to face the werewolf.

Unable to hold the ball any longer, she released it and a great breeze knocked over both Crystal and the werewolf.

Recovering quickly, Crystal rolled over on top of the werewolf, pinning it to the ground.

"Hurry, I can't hold her forever!" Crystal shouted using everything she could to keep it down.

"Ok, I got it! *Insolation*." Tiara raised her hand and a small ball of light formed in her palm. Without hesitation she threw it high into the sky and controlled it until it was in line with the moon, then it exploded. The night turned into day and the spell completely blocked out the moon.

Crystal looked back down at the werewolf and saw it was turning back into the girl, but she'd passed out.

"It's working! Can you hold the spell? I'll tie her up," Crystal said and then sprinted over to her horse for some rope as Tiara struggled to maintain the spell, crying out in pain.

"There, done, you can relax," Crystal said once she was confident the girl has been tied up securely. "Good job!" she said and fell back onto the ground, exhausted.

"Thanks, you too," Tiara said as she collapsed to her knees. Sweat had formed on her forehead from the exertion and so she took a minute to catch her breath. The sun in the sky faded as night returned with the full moon. The reappearance of full moon caused the girl to start shaking again and turn back into the werewolf.

"Strange, she's asleep. How did she change back?" Crystal asked pondering what happened.

"That is rare," Tiara said with a sense of melancholy.

"What do you mean?"

"For her to change like that means she was never bitten, or cursed or tormented by someone. Means she's always been like this."

"Can't something be done to stop her from changing," Crystal asked seeing the sadness in Tiara.

"Not unless we kill her. Though I imagine the town will do that for us," Tiara said, rubbing her neck wearily.

"She can't control who she is when she's the werewolf. That's not fair." she said trying to save her.

"We need the archers from this town. They're the best in the whole land. We need them for this rebellion to work, Tentaclous has been hesitant to invade here because of them" Tiara said plainly.

"We can't take her back, she'll die," Crystal protested.

"If we don't then the entire reason we came here is for nothing."

"Then we sacrifice an innocent life for our own goals."

"If we don't, we sacrifice everyone that fights for us."

"If there is a trial, she will be found guilty and be committed to death, the people won't let you excuse her," Crystal said, angrier now.

"As queen, I have the privilege of final say. We could use a good fighter like her. I'll tell her to work for our army in order to pay off her debt.

"She's too young to fight."

"We have little choice," Tiara replied sadly.

Crystal didn't reply and then nodded reluctantly.

"*Nare,*" Tiara said with a flick of her wrist and the werewolf girl rose from the ground to float in the air.

They turned and walked back toward their horses as the werewolf floated behind them.

They found the horses with their heads still in the apple tree and their mouths full to the brim with apples. They laughed.

"Hey, piglets, over here," Crystal said with a quick wave. Crystal's horse walked over to her, slow and lazy, fat from all the apples he'd eaten. She laughed and then mounted. Tiara jerked the reins of her Mustang to make him stand still and climbed into the saddle.

The sun rose in front of them as they wearily rode back to the city and, as they did so, the werewolf slowly turned back into the girl.

Chapter XX

Late to the Party

Morning and The Siren, Mudmucker, Noctremis, and the Grunting were on a hill that overlooking the partially ruined city of Ridgemont. People were toing and froing as they tried to rebuild their city. The burned catapults still smoked on the skyline and the barbarian camp had been ransacked. Not a trace of the barbarian army remained save for the fallen on the ground.

"Something's wrong. Where are all our forces?" Noctremis said as he looked over the battlefield.

"The princess must have been here. Look at those guards, nothing but armor and weapons. She must know magic, powerful magic," the Siren said, eyeing the armor and weapons patrolling the decayed streets.

The Mudmucker looked around at the dirt, got down on all fours and sniffed around. Then he tasted the dirt and quickly spat it back out quickly.

"Our forces were here. The tint of their armor is in the dirt. Can you beat the princess in a fight then, magically?" the Mudmucker asked looking at the Siren.

"Hard to tell without seeing her fight," the Grunting said matter-of-factly.

"These are permanent creatures, they don't have to be maintained by any spell, right?" the Mudmucker said, scratching his head and watching the empty armor and weapons patrol the streets.

"Correct, but I don't know how such a young person could cast a spell like this," the Siren said. "She wasn't trained by a human. Couldn't have been," There was a pause, and then she clenched her fist and said, "The dragon! He must have trained her, that is the only explanation" Saying with a breath of frustration.

The Siren looked at all the barbarian bodies around them.

"Look at these tracks their army is moving, we might be able to catch up to them," the Grunting said.

"No, we can't and shouldn't fight the princess if she is as powerful as I think she is. That would be foolish. Magic puts stress on your body, it strains it. Most human wizards who have been studying magic their whole lives can only cast and maintain a few Golems or just one of those empty armor warriors, and even then it would be temporary depending on the wizard. She cast enough for an entire town.

"She might be weak then, because of the spell," suggested the Grunting.

"I'm not taking that chance," the Siren declared, giving notice for the army following them to stop.

"They could have that dragon with them. Who knows what tricks he has up his sleeve?" Noctremis said aloud nervously.

Grunting walked over and pushed Mudmucker.

"Yeah, idiot," the Grunting said while glaring at the Mudmucker.

"An idiot, is I?" the Mudmucker growled as he picked up some mud and flung it in the Grunting's eyes.

"Mud flinger!" the Grunting shouted.

The Grunting grabbed Mudmucker, and they fell to the ground, wrestling.

The Siren ignored them, looking at the tracks in front of them and talked to Noctremis.

"Our best option would be to let our troops heal and rest until the final battle. That way they will be fresh," she said, looking back to the army behind them.

"True, there is nothing more we can do here," Noctremis said with a nod.   "Enough!" the Siren yelled at the Mudmucker and Grunting, still fighting on the ground after they had interrupted a thought she had. "Everyone march toward the capital!" she yelled out in frustration to the troops.

"Call it a draw," the Grunting whispered to the Mudmucker.

"For now." the Mudmucker whispered back softly, trying to keep the Siren from hearing.

Noctremis laughed at them and then hurried to catch up to the Siren who was now marching ahead.

The army had changed course, and at the Siren's command began to march toward the Capital where King Tentaclous waited.

"King Tentaclous will be angry," the Siren said muttered to herself while rubbing her neck.

"We will tell him of the princess's power and he'll show us mercy," Noctremis said with a shrug of his shoulders.

"Reeet! Tentaclous give mercy?" the Grunting squealed at noctremis's thought.

"I think he's going to turn us into a stew," the Mudmucker said unafraid to show fear.

"Maybe, we should run for it?" Noctremis suggested.

"There is nowhere we can hide. At least with Tentaclous we stand a chance," the Siren said to end the conversation.

The four of them putt around behind the army. The Siren was the only one not afraid of King Tentaclous's fury. She pushed the others to make sure everyone continued to walk forward. Though fights still broke out from time to time as they ever so slowly moved back to the capital.

Chapter XXI

Second Chances

Crystal and Tiara arrived back in Grand Amour to the cheering of its people as they entered the city, but the cheers soon turned into boos as they threw lettuce and tomatoes at the tied up werewolf girl. The crowd became more violent the closer they came to the town's center and then someone tried to attack her.

The attacker jumped forward out of the crowd and started to beat her. Tiara quickly pulled the girl into her arms and made a beeline toward the entrance of the Capital building. They jumped off their horses and ploughed through the front door, quickly closing and locking it behind them.

Tiara returned the werewolf girl to her floating position in mid-air and entered the study with Crystal to where Count Aldéric and Charlotte were.

"We've found the werewolf that plagues your town," Tiara announced. Count Aldéric and Charlotte looked up from the books they were reading.

"Don't you guys ever do anything other than read?" Crystal asked after she saw that they were reading books still.

"We do the town's taxes in here as well." Count Aldéric said as he adjusted the glasses on his nose. "They usually take a bit of time."

"Is that girl the werewolf?" asked Charlotte, pointing to the floating girl. "It can't be. She's just a girl, and is far too young. You've made a mistake." Charlotte said without a moments second thought.

Count Aldéric looked at the unconscious young girl for a moment. "She is awfully young," he added.

"She transformed right in front of us," Crystal protested with her voice slightly louder than before.

"She was right where you said she would be. She transformed and then attacked us," Tiara said firmly.

Their conversation was interrupted by the wolf girl who began to stir and then opened her eyes still dizzy from the transformation.

"What? Why am I tied up?" she asked, struggling to get free until she saw that she was floating. "What's happening here? I blacked out again? I'm innocent!" The girl shook her head and tried to compose herself.

"Yes, and it's also very convenient for the guilty party to lose their memory. Don't try to plead innocent," Tiara scowled at the wolf girl, not believing her..

"I have no memory of last night."

Tiara retracted her flotation spell and lowered the girl to the ground.

"The transformation might have a few lingering symptoms?" Crystal asked unsure whether she believed her or not.

"You have no memory of last night? What about yesterday morning or afternoon?" Count Aldéric asked inquisitively to the wolf girl.

"I was in the orchard," she replied, looking down at the floor.

"What happens when you look at the full moon?" Crystal asked with a shrug of her shoulders to Tiara.

"I don't know. I feel kind of funny, then I start to tingle is the last sensation that I remember,"

"Is that all you remember?" Tiara asked.

The wolf girl nodded.

"Why were you hiding?" Crystal asked with a rub to her chin.

"Last time I was here, everyone seemed so angry at me, but I wasn't sure why so I ran away." The werewolf girl pleaded.

"So you blacked out, last night? What's the last thing you can remember?" Tiara asked.

"I...I don't know. I remember being in the woods, but that's all, I swear!" the werewolf girl begged and fell to her knees.

"Does this happen only every so often, like once a month?" Tiara asked.

"I black out every once in a while. Around evening, I guess."

"If she blacks out then she wouldn't be in control of herself during that time. I'd say if she remembered, that would be different," Crystal said.

"I agree," Tiara said with a sigh.

Outside the crowd rumbled and started to get louder. Charlotte walked over and looked out the window, then turned back to everyone else. "I've heard enough to decree that she is our werewolf. The people outside need an answer; they are growing restless." Charlotte whispered as she kept her voice hushed when she was near the balcony.

"She's so young, though. Is there a magical cure for her?" Count Aldéric asked.

"That depends. Were you ever bitten by a wolf?" Tiara asked turning to the wolf girl with a raised eyebrow.

"No. I've had the black outs ever since I can remember."

Tiara looked at the girl for a moment, her mind ticking over.

"What does that mean?" Crystal asked.

"It means either her mother or her father was a werewolf and it's kind of bred into her. It's part of her, so she's either got to learn to somehow control it or continue letting it control her and face the consequences," Tiara said looking into the werewolf girl's eyes.

The girl nervously glanced from Tiara to Crystal.

"Maybe Tarragon knows a way?" Crystal asked, trying to think of a solution.

"He taught me how to cure a werewolf's bite. I don't think there is a cure for her, just as there is no way to make someone immortal, well no healthy way at least," Tiara said as she hinted toward vampirism with a finger pointing to a tooth.

"You could take her with you," Charlotte suggested with another glance out the balcony window. "Although the people might be angry, it would be better for her."

"Yes, and it would help rally the people by showing them you can and will help deal with the problems of our people," Count Aldéric said as if like he was preparing a speech in his head.

Nobody spoke as Tiara considered the suggestion. "Sure, we'll take her with us."

"We'll need a spare horse," Crystal said, looking to Charlotte and Count Aldéric.

They both nodded.

"Of course," Charlotte replied. She summoned a servant and asked him to fetch a horse from the stables.

Crystal Leaned down and extended her hand to the werewolf girl. "The name's Crystal," she said with a goofy smile.

"Amy," replied the wolf girl with a small smile. "Can I be untied?" the werewolf girl said while lifting her hands and looking down to her feet.

"Oh, yes," Tiara said with a laugh. She made a quick gesture with her hand and the ropes fell away.

"I'm sorry; I haven't talked to anyone in a long time," Amy said to Crystal with a forced smile.

"Oh, what about your parents, brothers, sisters, family?" Crystal asked.

"I don't remember," Amy said.

"You remember who they were, though? Did they just disappear one night?" Crystal tried to clarify.

"I don't have any brothers or sisters as far as I know. And I've never met my parents. Am I going to die?"

"N-," Crystal started to answer but then cut herself off and looked to Tiara, "My queen?"

"No, she is not. We will take her with us and silence the crowd outside." She moved to the balcony where the city's people had gathered.

"Careful on what you say, one wrong word and we'll have a full-fledged riot on our hands," Charlotte said quietly.

"Yes, tell them that she will undergo 'Military Justice' and that her condition is a disease and that you're taking her to see if there is a cure," Count Aldéric said sitting in the chair behind his desk.

"Sure," Tiara said, suddenly feeling nervous listened and replied with a nod of her head. "Don't open those doors yet, let's go over to the balcony" Charlotte said softly and stood up as she reached the balcony window.

They stepped out onto the balcony that overlooked the town's center. The crowd quickly silenced as Tiara and Charlotte came into view of the people.

"People of Grand Amour, I have found your werewolf. She is a young girl with a disease that can be magically cured. After learning that the crimes she committed were only under influence of the disease, I will force her to work off her misdeeds once she is cured. By the power vested in me by my parents, the king and queen of Abbigonia, I give you my word that the werewolf threat is gone," Tiara said as loudly and as clearly as she could manage.

The crowd outside began to rumble as the people debated whether she had done the right thing. Tiara walked back inside and everyone clapped as the crowd outside started to cheer once more.

"You guys should leave," Charlotte said with a sweeping motion toward the door.

"Welcome back, my queen," Count Aldéric said with a humble smile. "Our archers will be with you when you need them."

They walked through the Capital building to the entrance where they first entered. "Good bye you guys. Remember Mayor Tomwell's town in the central part of the forest" Tiara said with a final wave and went to get on her horse. "Meet up with us there," Crystal said, pulling out a map and pointing to the location of Mayor Tomwell's town.

"In the forest?" Charlotte asked unfamiliar with the town of Krylon.

"There is a secret city there led by a man called Mayor Tomwell," Tiara said.

"Be careful, my lady. Not all the people in this kingdom would like your return," Count Aldéric warned with a finger to the side of his nose.

"I understand and thank you," Tiara said.

They walked back out into the streets and mounted their horses as one was pulled and around for Amy.

"Would you like to stay the night?" Charlotte asked feeling exhaustion start to take over.

"No, we have a lot to do and we need to keep moving to stay ahead of Tentaclous," Tiara replied as she nudged the Mustang forward.

"Are you the prophesized queen?" Amy asked, following closely behind them.

"Yes, yes, I am. But you can call me Tiara," she replied with a smile. "Would you like to join the resistance?" Tiara asked already thinking she didn't have much choice.

"Of course," Amy replied. The three of them stopped at the jewelry store on the way out of town as Tiara had promised. Crystal was like a child at Christmas morning running through the store. She was trying on a menagerie of necklaces and rings and crowns. Amy looked at some rubies and emeralds and sapphires and Tiara looked around and tried to match her necklace with something. The people that worked at the jewelry store tried to sell them everything. Then the three of them rode out of town on their horses. Amy was almost on top of Tiara's horse, she followed her closely. The people celebrated as they left. The sun was almost on top of the sky.

Chapter XXII

Outskirts of
Meadowvale

Triskelon and Chasten traveled through the old forest with Mistral leading the way. He sniffed around and navigated through the winding paths of the seemingly endless forest. Chasten and Triskelon blindly followed the wolf, not even paying attention to where they were going.

The road was narrow from the dense, lush forest that closed in around the pathway until it suddenly opened up as they came into a wide field sparsely dotted with trees.

"There's an encampment ahead with a collection of horses," Mistral said, sniffing the air.

"That must be it" Chasten said pointing to a distant collection of tents that could be seen far out in the middle of the field.

"There's nothing else around for miles," Triskelon said, hoping they weren't completely lost.

They approached the encampment slowly and as more of it became visible, they could see a series of tents and temporary buildings filled with knights that were jousting. There were more people hanging around looking extremely bored, amusing themselves however they can.

"Hello, who's in charge here?" Chasten called out blatantly as they came closer.

"Who's asking?" a knight yelled back sarcastically.

"Chasten the legendary warrior of Abbigonia." Chasten said with a puffed out chest and fists at his hips.

"And Triskelon the legendary spell luminator of Abbigonia." Triskelon lifted his hand up into the air and let a small ball of moonlight drift up from his palm.

Mistral shook his head and chuckled.

Some people looked around at them and then went back to what they were doing. Chasten, Triskelon and Mistral entered the encampment only to be greeted by a tall and imposing knight.

"What brings you three here?" he asked.

"The queen, she has returned and is gathering forces," Triskelon said, suddenly realizing they had no way of proving this claim.

"She calls for you to join her. But we need to hurry, will you ride with us?" Chasten asked as he reached out a hand. The knight looked confused at first and then nodded.

"Ok, let's get to it then," he said with a soft chuckle.

"Really?" Triskelon asked, shocked.

"Of course not, unless you can prove it."

"Sweet! I can prove it" Chasten said and began searching his armor for something.

"No, you can't," Triskelon said.

"I can too. You see this burn mark on my armor? It isn't a normal burn mark, is it?" Chasten said, pointing it out to both of them. The knight looked at the burn mark on Chasten's chest piece and then gave him an incredulous look.

"I guess not," he said, humoring him.

"Yup, that's because it's from a bolt of lightning. Now you and I both know that it takes a lot of magical power to summon lightning, right? The queen was being trained by Tarragon, the king's dragon, so she could one day return and retake the kingdom. So, the only person in the kingdom strong enough to cause a mark like this must be either the kings dragon Tarragon or Tiara," Chasten said with a happy smile and a re-extended hand.

"Hey, I thought I made that mark," Triskelon said remembering there encounter in the cave.

"Shut up, stupid," Chasten hissed.

"Oh," Triskelon muttered to himself.

"Well, few people know the name of the king's dragon. And even fewer know the princess's real name. Captain Ruhk told me one day this might happen." The knight turned around and started to shout to everyone, "All right boys, let's pack up. The princess has returned and we're going to war." Everyone stopped and looked at the knight before cheering loudly.

"I can't believe that worked," Chasten said as his jaw dropped as he heard the whole town cheer.

"I knew it would," Triskelon nodded confidently with a slap to Chasten's back.

"We did it!" Chasten said, the moment finally hitting him.

"Heroes, baby!" Triskelon yelled out.

The small encampment quickly packed up within a few hours.

"Lead the way, heroes," the knight said.

"I don't even... never mind," Mistral said, shaking his head in disbelief and turning around to show them the way.

The knight blinked. "I will never touch a drop of whiskey again. That wolf talked," he said to Chasten.

"Yeah, he does that. But he's a good navigator so we'll be fine."

"Sure," muttered the knight. "By the way, my name is Sir Yuri," he said, holding out a hand.

"Great to meet you, Sir Yuri," said Chasten, shaking his hand.

"Where are we headed?"

"To Mayor Tomwell's town," Triskelon replied.

"Who?" Sir Yuri asked and looked to his knights to see if they knew who that was.

"It's a secret town in the middle of the forest. Everyone is meeting there. Lead the way Mistral," Chasten said, pointing to the forest.

"I've seen stranger things happen, I suppose," Mistral said to himself. He broke into a run and everyone else followed close behind. The whole encampment moved with them as they went back into the forest. Triskelon and Chasten smirked following close behind.

Chapter XXIII

Pirates of The Lost Harbor

Tarragon and Captain Ruhk flew through the clouds and over a town made almost entirely from wood. It was a port town, and the ocean water splashed over the sides of the docks as the whole town creaked in the wind. Molded spots covered the ends of the dock where water continuously splashed against the wood. Ships were in the port with people packing and carrying boxes on and off the different vessels. The buildings in the town stood irregularly and were made from discarded ship parts.

Tarragon picked out a slightly open area on the wooden path and began his descent.

"All right, you remember that human image spell?" Captain Ruhk said as they swooped closer to the town.

"Yes, it's *homo* something. *Homo forma? Homo...*" Tarragon said trying to remember.

"Just stay here and try to keep out of trouble. I will look for Dame Eclipse," Captain Ruhk said as Tarragon landed on the outskirts of the town.

"All right, I'll be around," Tarragon said, curling up on the grass where he'd landed.

Captain Ruhk looked around for a minute to get his bearings. The few people that had seen Tarragon land were now staring at him.

"I suppose I the tavern should be around here," Captain Ruhk said with a shrug of his shoulders.

"Yeah, everyone of any importance will be there, knowing how pirates work," Tarragon muttered eyeing back the people who were staring at him.

"I hope Dame Eclipse made it here," Captain Ruhk said. He set off down a side street and it wasn't long until he found what he was looking for.

As he walked through the door of the Tavern, everyone stopped and looked at him. After a few seconds, everyone turned around and went about their business. Dame Eclipse walked over from the corner where she had been sat at a table.

"Captain Ruhk, this is a nice surprise," Dame Eclipse breathed with a smile and a nodding gesture to follow her.

"Dame Eclipse, the pleasure is all mine, mi-lady" Captain Ruhk replied with a warm smile.

"I'll introduce you to the Admiral," Dame Eclipse said as they walked back over to her corner table where Admiral Stevens waited.

"Admiral Stevens, this is Captain Ruhk," Dame Eclipse introduced them.

"Pleased to meet you," Captain Ruhk said as he and Dame Eclipse sat down at the table.

"Dame Eclipse tells me you will let us raid the castle and keep whatever we want?"

"If your ships can make it there before the battle and effectively cut off the royal harbor from sea-bound supplies and reinforcement."

"My ships are the fastest in all the seas. If anyone can make it there in time, it would be my fleet. You are smart to come to me," he replied with a toothy grin.

"Yes, about your fleet. How reliable are your pirates and swashbucklers? If king Tentaclous has a navy, will your ships tuck tail and run?" Captain Ruhk asked.

"My ships are reliable enough. And experienced; we've been raiding port towns all around here. Barbarians don't scare my men," Admiral Stevens replied.

"We don't want just your experienced men. We want all of your ships. We want you to sail the whole fleet, everything thing you have," Captain Ruhk replied impatiently.

"Of course. But what if your castle is void of loot? My men don't work for free, Captain." Admiral Stevens replied still trying to get more money from them.

"Come on, Admiral, I thought your pirates were blood thirsty, swashbuckling, warmongers like the old dime novels my daughter used to read," Captain Ruhk replied with a smile.

"And I always lives up to my reputation," Admiral Stevens replied with a laugh.

"Well, those are the pirates the queen needs." Captain Ruhk stated his smile slowly fading.

"Ah, then you've named someone queen. I would like to meet her before I make a decision." Admiral Stevens chalked up as another price he needed.

"The queen is the daughter of the old king and queen. She has returned to restore the balance. She is busy and doesn't have time to come here to chat with you," Captain Ruhk said, feeling the frustration build.

"Ah, a pity, perhaps after the battle then." Admiral Stevens replied as if he never wanted to meet her.

"That would require that you to actually stay and fight. Looting and running doesn't merit a meeting with the queen," Dame Eclipse replied sternly.

"The experienced men and I will stay and fight. The new recruits I have less control over," Admiral Stevens finally said.

"If I know our king, you can expect quite a fight. If they want any loot, they'll have to fight through his forces first," Dame Eclipse said.

"Well, I just won't tell the men that then. Very well then for the queen's sake. You have my ships at your disposal. But how I command my men is my business."

"Well then, when your ships are ready, make sail as soon as possible," Captain Ruhk said.

"I want a guarantee I'll receive payment of some sort," Admiral Stevens scolded looking from one to the other.

"The princess will compensate you upon victory," Captain Ruhk said brusquely.

"So when is this battle?" Admiral Stevens asked with a raised eyebrow.

"As soon as everyone meets up at Mayor Tomwell's city, we will need enough time to gather our forces and co-ordinate an attack. Then we die for something we believe in," Captain Ruhk said with a final nod.

"I assume this location is a few days' ride away?" Admiral Stevens asked, starting to calculate how many days it will take to sail there in his head.

"By horse, yes but we will travel by a dragon. Everyone else should already be their when we arrive," Captain Ruhk said with a quick glance around him.

"All right, I'll make my ships ready to leave and I'll see you on the battlefield." Admiral Stevens replied picking up some scrolls he had next to him.

Admiral Stevens shook hands with Captain Ruhk and then Dame Eclipse before leaving the tavern.

"Has the queen really returned?" Dame Eclipse asked in a whisper.

"Yes, war is upon us. We will meeting her at Mayor Tomwell's town."

"He's not on our side," Dame Eclipse said with a worried look on her face.

"What?" Captain Ruhk suddenly stopped and a look of panicked flickered across his face.

"That spineless coward, Tomwell, would never allow a rebellion to organize in his town." Dame Eclipse said loudly to make sure Captain Ruhk would hear her.

"Tarragon and Tiara were pretty sure that he was with us," Captain Ruhk said.

They scurried out the Tavern and once they were in the street; they broke into a run toward Tarragon.

"We'll find out, eventually. Tarragon!" Dame Eclipse shouted. Dame Eclipse ran over to Tarragon and threw her arms around his neck as Tarragon put a hand on her back. "It's been a while but we haven't got time. We need to go to Mayor Tomwell's town now," she said.

"Are we not staying here tonight? I'm exhausted," Tarragon said with a yawn.

"Tomwell is a traitor, he's not safe," Captain Ruhk said getting Dame Eclipse and himself onto Tarragon's back.

"If I fly anymore, my heart could stop."

"Okay, okay," said Captain Ruhk, giving Tarragon a gentle pat.

Tarragon stretched, then looked up to the sky as storm clouds gathered.

"I hope they're okay."

"You trained her, right? And I trained Crystal. They'll be fine. And they should have a few armies with them," Captain Ruhk reassured him as he looked up to the sky.

Tarragon nodded. "Tiara is all that is best in me. She can handle herself; we will just have to hurry in the morning." Tarragon said as he watched the storm clouds above them get ready to burst.

"If you two are sure," Dame Eclipse said with a worried look.

"*Homo forma parvus,*" Tarragon blurted remembering the image spell and shape-shifted into his human form.

"Let's find a place to stay for the night," Captain Ruhk said as a loud clash of thunder burst from the sky.

"I have a bad feeling," Dame Eclipse whispered.

"I could ride a horse in this form," Tarragon suggested.

"It's all right, Tarragon. You're right, you need rest, we all do. Crystal is more than capable of protecting Tiara," Captain Ruhk said with faith in his daughter. "Besides, there's no way we can ride through this storm." Captain Ruhk intoned moving toward edge of town where the water was. The three of them stood side by side at the water's edge. There was a hand railing as they watched what they could see of the sunset. The clouds were heavy with rain as lightning began to streak across the sky as night time came.

Chapter XXIV

Allies with Evil

The sun barely peaked over the edges of the trees as the ground in Mayor Tomwell's small town of Krylon started to shake. The town's people gathered in the small town square to see what was happening.

Captain Clod and his men marched through the tree line and carved a path through the woods and into the center of town in an unorganized mess. The company came to a stop and Captain Clod addressed the people, "Who is Tomwell?"

"I-I am him", Mayor Tomwell replied nervously.

"I am Captain Clod, commander of all the king's armies. Where did this *queen* go?" he spat.

"She said she would return, when she'd gathered her army," Mayor Tomwell confessed.

"When?" Clod asked, gripping his axe tightly in his hand.

"I-I don't know. Soon?"

Captain Clod took a few steps toward the Mayor and grabbed his tunic on both sides, easily lifting him off the ground.

"She had better come back. If you dragged me out here on a wild goose chase, there will be consequences. You have until nightfall, or the mystery queen won't be the one under the guillotine, you hear me?!"

Mayor Tomwell nodded furiously and Captain Clod threw him to the ground. The barbarian Captain looked at the buildings around them and suddenly came up with an idea.

"All of my men, I want you inside these buildings, now! Don't leave a trace," he commanded. Clod's men entered the buildings, pushing everyone out of their own homes and forcing the town's people into the street. Captain Clod looked back to Mayor Tomwell with a smile.

"Have your men continue life as normal. If your queen returns before nightfall, we'll catch her. And you'll be a rich man," he said before following his men into the nearest building.

It left a worried Mayor Tomwell standing in the middle of the town square with his people looking at him.

"You heard the Captain, continue life as normal," he said with a nervous swallow. Everyone slowly started to go about their business as usual whilst the Mayor Tomwell stood in the center of town and waited, unsure what to do with himself. He finally let out a long sigh.

"Impatient barbarians. I need you to come back now girl. It has been too soon" Mayor Tomwell sweats profusely and looked to the forest tree line hoping for something to happen. The sun continued to rise into the sky and people seem to temporarily forget that Captain Clod hide inside, all except Mayor Tomwell who stood nervously in the center of town. He looked to the tree line and wished for Tiara to return to them.

Chapter XXV

Surprise!

High Noon at Mayor Tomwell's town and Mayor Tomwell still stood in the middle of town. Mayor Tomwell closed his eyes and looked up toward the sun. He whispered to himself.

"Someone come into town. Anyone I can blame this on" Tomwell whispered to himself, nervously tapping his side and gazing at the forest's tree line.

"What am I going to do?" he muttered to himself, with every passing minute, the knot in his stomach grew tighter.

Suddenly, three girls riding horses came into view on the forest track. Mayor Tomwell watched with relief as they rode into the town. He opened his arms to them as they entered the town.

Before the Mayor could formally welcome them, commotion behind him made him turn to see a man dressed in armor, riding a horse and leading a troop of men who wearily trudged into his town from the other side.

"Excuse me, who are you?" Mayor Tomwell asked already trying to shoo Duke Hardloff from the town.

"Duke Hardloff of Ridgemont."

"What are you doing here? You can't be here."

"We are here for the revolution," replied the Duke. "Now, get out of my way, Mayor, before I make an example out of you. I only take orders from the queen," he said as he pushed past him.

"Welcome," Mayor Tomwell muttered to himself as he watched the Duke approach the three girls. Mayor Tomwell had no choice but to let him inside the city. Tiara, Crystal and Amy walked to the center of town and hopped down off of their horses. Duke Hardloff walked up to them.

"You must be Tiara?" Duke Hardloff said, taking his helmet off and gesturing to the glowing ruby necklace.

"Yes, I am and I'm pleased to meet you" Tiara said as she shook Hardloff's hand.

"Duke Hardloff of Ridgemont, milady. The honor is all mine." Duke Hardloff said with his chest puffed out and confidence written on his face.

"Corporal Crystal, her majesty's personal escort," Crystal said, pulling up alongside Tiara and looking down at Hardloff, eyeing the emblem on his armor before extending a hand to welcome him.

"Names Amy, fugitive and wanted by both King Tentaclous and the true princess" Amy said with a smirk and a hand on her hip.

"Pleased to meet you, Crystal. Have you heard from Captain Ruhk yet?" Duke Hardloff asked momentarily looking around and then back to the girls.

Before Tiara could reply Amy pointed down the pathway as Mistral, Chasten and Triskelon arrived with Sir Yuri and his knights.

"Well, looks like we have more visitors," Mayor Tomwell huffed and shook his head in disbelief.

"I don't believe it," Tiara said in shock, her jaw dropped to the ground.

"I told you they'd come through," Crystal said with a smirk.

"They have a wolf," Amy said with a fascinated gaze, staring at Mistral and then looked at the town's people; none of them had taken any notice of the mass arrival of strangers and continued work. She looked around at the empty buildings, noticing that not even the elderly were in their homes.

"Something's wrong," she muttered, narrowing her eyes at the town.

"What?" Tiara asked as she looked around and noticed it too.

Mayor Tomwell held his breath and suddenly the silence was broken by Captain Clod's shouts, "Now! Swarm the one with the necklace! Charge!"

Barbarians stormed out of the building and charged toward Tiara. The rest of the army poured out of the buildings like a wave of destruction.

"Lock shields! Protect the queen!" cried Duke Hardloff as his men formed a tight circle around Tiara, locking their shields and drawing their weapons. The barbarians clashed against the Duke's men who were weary and struggled to maintain their formation.

Captain Clod appeared from one building and watched the battle.

"Perfect timing, Captain Clod," Duke Hardloff said to himself.

"Who?" Amy asked.

"Captain Clod, his strength is past legendary. He is unmatched by anyone except the king himself," the Duke said as his sword clashed against that of a barbarian's. "He's the King's right hand."

"The one with the glowing red necklace is the queen. I want her alive!" yelled out Captain Clod as his men broke Duke Hardloff's line. Suddenly, vines erupted from the ground, entangling some barbarians, slowing them down.

"Is that all you can do?" Crystal called out, watching the barbarian's rip through the vines. "Where's the fire and brimstone?!"

"It's the only idea I have right now." Tiara said, feeling panicked as her eyes were locked on the battlefield.

"Make the moon come out and I can help," Amy shouted in a panic.

"But you can't control it," Tiara replied, trying to think of a spell she could use.

"Make it rain fire!" Crystal yelled out.

"We are in the middle of a forest, we'd be trapped!" Tiara yelled back.

"Chasten, look!" Triskelon said from the other side of the battlefield as he sent a ball of flame into several barbarians, setting them alight.

"Tiara's in there!" Chasten yelled out.

"To arms, lads! They were true to their word, now the queen needs our help," Sir Yuri called out as he unsheathed his sword.

His knights drew their swords and charged without hesitation into the middle of the battle, driving the barbarians back and allowing Duke Hardloff's men to regroup.

Mistral and the others watched for a moment.

Chasten and Triskelon looked at each other. Chasten drew his sword whilst Triskelon adjusted the grip on his staff.

"Eternus Vir!" they yelled in unison.

They began to run into the thick of the battle, calling out, "Vivat Regina!"

"Fascinating motto, we really must discuss it later," Mistral said with a shake of his head and followed them into the fray.

Captain Clod watched the battle in front of him, and he wasn't happy.

"If you want something done, you have to do it yourself," he snapped and charged into the battle toward Tiara.

He swung at one of Duke Hardloff's soldiers, easily knocking him head over heels. Swinging again, Duke Hardloff suddenly appeared through the mass of bodies and attacked. Clod parried his attack and swung at him, knocking him back.

Before he could deliver a final blow, Crystal swung at Clod, halting his advance a moment then with a snarl, Clod swung at her, their weapons clashing as she defended herself. Clod used his strength and height to push their weapons higher, forcing Crystal to move her arms above her head. He quickly shoved her with all his strength, pushing Crystal onto her back. He swung his sword high only to find himself blocked by Duke Hardloff. Clod pushed down on the sword, forcing the Duke lower and lower. Buckling under the weight of the barbarian, Duke Hardloff fell to his knees. He lifted his sword up for one final swing when a fireball hit him square on the shoulder, throwing off his aim.

Looking up, Clod saw Tiara and smiled. Stricken with fear and unable to move, Tiara stared back.

Amy, seeing Tiara motionless, looked at Clod, then back to her queen.

Without hesitation, Amy jumped behind Clod and punched between the shoulder blades, which barely scratched him. Then she jumped back quickly. Surprised, Clod turned around and looked at Amy who was already letting her wolf's instincts take over.

"You're stronger than you look, child" said Captain Clod with a confident smile.

Clod swung toward Amy but she easily dodged the attack.

Tiara threw another fireball, but it wasn't enough to distract Clod from his new target.

Amy made opportunistic attacks and got low to the ground and tried to find her next place to attack when Clod suddenly kicked the ground, knocking dirt into Amy's eyes and blinded her long enough for Clod to pick her up and throw her over the heads of his barbarian army. Amy hit the solid ground hard but didn't get back up.

Seeing Amy on the ground, Tiara summoned a fireball the size of her torso and launched it at Clod. Realizing he didn't have time to dodge it, Clod let the fireball hit him and shrugged it off as he grabbed Tiara's throat, lifting her up with one hand. Tiara grabbed hold of his hand, desperate to get free and shook, terrified with fear her eyes grew huge as her feet could no longer touch the ground. Just then Yuri and the others charged once more into the battlefield and cut a swath into Clod's men. Clod looked over to Mayor Tomwell who was about to turn around and run like a rat who deserted a sinking ship.

"Mayor Tomwell, let's go. The queen is ours! Retreat! Everyone back to the castle!" Captain Clod shouted while carrying Tiara aloft for all to see.

The barbarian Captain strode through his men still fighting and grabbed hold of Mayor Tomwell by the scruff of his neck, forcing him to walk. As Captain Clod retreated from the town, his army followed. They left only a few barbarians fighting as more of them fled the scene.

Chasten frantically looked around for Tiara before finally spotting her with Clod's hand still around her neck.

"My queen!" Chasten yelled out.

"Chas, no! Wait!" Triskelon shouted to his friend who was already charging in.

Chasten charged through Clod's men and launched himself from his horse, tackling Clod to the ground as he fell. Both of them rolled, stood up and squared off against one another. Tiara, temporarily freed from Clods grasped, started to summon a fireball, only to be grabbed by Clod's men.

Clod raised his weapon and swung at Chasten who quickly raised his shield to block the attack but was knocked off of his feet by the force of the blow. Before Chasten could retaliate, a barbarian bonked him on the head and knocked him unconscious.

"Take him, too. An extra prize for the king," Captain Clod said.

Captain Clod, Mayor Tomwell and Clod's army disappeared into the forest with Tiara and Chasten.

The small town was torn asunder from the battle. Sir Yuri and Triskelon looked at each other with a worried face as Duke Hardloff, Crystal and Amy recovered from their barbarian encounters.

"They took Chasten and Tiara," Triskelon said in a panicked voice.

"Tend to our wounded," Mistral commanded. "We will wait for Captain Ruhk to return. Sir Yuri, will you patrol the perimeter?"

"Of course. Keep a sharp eye out, men call out if anyone approaches," Sir Yuri told his men as he himself also went on patrol.

Mistral began to sniff around the bodies that littered the ground, looking for those who were alive but wounded.

Triskelon rode and ran over to where Crystal lay on the ground. He took out his flask of water and offered it to her. Mistral walked over to Amy and sniffed her.

"Even this girl was hurt in the battle" Triskelon said with a shake of his head.

"Trisk? What happened?" Crystal muttered, still hazy from the fight.

Triskelon swallowed hard and had trouble answering her, "They took Tiara and Chasten. No word yet from Captain Ruhk or Tarragon."

Triskelon helped Crystal to her feet as Mistral gave Amy a lick on her cheek and nudged her with his nose.

"Is she dead?" Crystal asked looking down at her.

"No, she's alive. Look, she's coming to," Mistral said and took a few steps back.

Amy opened her eyes slowly then jumped to her feet quickly ready for battle again.

"Easy now, you've just been through a lot," Mistral said wagging his tail and pretending to be very friendly.

"We're on your side," Triskelon said when she didn't back down.

"Amy, it's cool. There with us," Crystal said.

Amy gave a nod and relaxed.

"I haven't lost a fight in a while," said Duke Hardloff, getting to his feet and rubbing his head. "I guess that Captain Clod shouldn't be underestimated."

"That big guy was Clod?" Crystal asked in shock at seeing the enormous barbarians.

"Yes."

"He might be big and strong, but he's clumsy and slow," said Amy. "I think I can beat him."

"Looks like he got the better of all of us," said Triskelon. "I'm sorry, we came in as soon as we could."

"This wasn't your fault, Trisk," Crystal said.

"Mayor Tomwell betrayed us. He must have told the king about Tiara," Duke Hardloff said.

"And then the king sent his best man to get her," Mistral said.

"Without her, the different cities armies won't work together. Without her, its over," Duke Hardloff said. "There's no point in even having a final battle to attack the castle."

"Because no one can work together longs enough to make a difference?" Triskelon said figuring out what the Duke was talking about.

"What do we do?" Amy asked waiting for someone to answer.

"It's not over," Crystal whispered before turning and walking away from the group. Triskelon watched her as she covered her eyes with a gloved hand. He followed and placed a hand on her shoulder.

"You're right. It's not over. We will figure something out; I promise. Don't think we've given up," Triskelon said reassuringly.

"Once they get to the castle, there will be no way to get them back. Tentaclous won't keep them for long," Crystal said through her tears.

"Incoming! Dragon and multiple riders!" yelled a patrolling knight. Within seconds, Tarragon came into view. He circled the town and quickly landed. Captain Ruhk and Dame Eclipse jumped off Tarragon's back and ran to the group.

"What's happened?! Crystal! Are you all right?" Captain Ruhk asked. Seeing his daughter in tears, he put a hand to her cheek and then placed both hands on her shoulders.

"Dad, Mayor Tomwell betrayed us, Clod was here, he took Tiara and Chasten," she said between sobs.

"Its okay, it's okay," he replied, pulling her into his embrace.

"Captain Ruhk, once again, you're a site for sore eyes," Duke Hardloff said with a smile.

Captain Ruhk let go of Crystal to shake hands with the Duke.

"We need to meet again after this, Hardloff, just so we can have a pleasant greeting," Captain Ruhk said with a smile, trying to lighten the mood.

"Dame Eclipse, a pleasure to see you alive," the Duke said, turning to Dame Eclipse. "I thought you'd died years ago."

"I thought they had burnt you and your city to the ground," she replied.

Tarragon walked over, scanning the group.

"Where's Tiara?" he asked.

"A dragon? You're cute, old guy," Amy said with a giggle.

"Cute?" Tarragon asked with a frown.

"Clod has her," Crystal said.

"What?" Tarragon said, outraged. Small puffs of smoke curled up from his nostrils.

"Any word yet from Count Aldéric?" Captain Ruhk asked looking around.

"We are here," came a voice. The group turned to see Count Aldéric, a platoon of footmen and another platoon of archers step out of the forest.

"Count Aldéric, welcome to our nightmare," Duke Hardloff said.

"Nightmare? What's happened?" Count Aldéric asked looking around at the dead bodies lying in the town's square.

"Ruhk, if Captain Clod gets Tiara back to the castle-" hissed Tarragon, suddenly interrupted by Sir Yuri riding up to the group.

"Captain Ruhk, my horses are the finest in the kingdom, we can catch up to Captain Clod," he said with a hurrying hand gesture.

"But there's no guarantee you'll be able to bring them back," Mistral said not wanting to ride off in a hurry to battle again.

"We are the best knights in the kingdom, if anyone can bring them back, it will be us," Sir Yuri said with a confident nod.

"My archers could take them all out without even getting close," Count Aldéric suggested.

"My foot soldiers are experienced and battle hardened. We would have just as much a chance to bring them in," Duke Hardloff said standing up proudly.

"Enough, all of you. Fact is, we need a plan. If we rush into battle, we invite the possibility of losing more men," Captain Ruhk said to silence everyone.

"Whatever we do, we need to do it quickly. Clod won't be wasting time," Dame Eclipse said, adjusting her armor.

"If I know Clod, he'll be already halfway back to the castle," Duke Hardloff said.

"We can't just let them go!" Crystal said picking up her weapon. "Sir Yuri, let's ride and go get her."

"Stop. Corporal you will not do such a thing, not without my orders. I am the ranking officer here now, so that makes me in command. No one does anything without my orders, got that?" Captain Ruhk said, pointing a finger at each of them before finally looking at Crystal.

"Captain, if we wait, we condemn them to death," Crystal said, not backing down.

"Corporal?" the Captain said, with a hard emphasis.

"Yes, sir," she muttered, finally relenting.

"If you charge into battle now, you condemn yourself along with them," Captain Ruhk reproached.

"What do we do?" Mistral asked.

"Mistral, you track them down. Duke Hardloff, Sir Yuri, Count Aldéric, and Dame Eclipse will come with me on a secret rescue mission," Captain Ruhk said making himself ready.

"I can track," said Amy. "Probably better than that old wolf. I'll be able to keep up easier, too."

"No, only we old experienced people are going. Everyone that is going has done this sort of thing before so we know what we're doing. The rest of you are to stay here, tend to our wounded and prepare for war," Captain Ruhk said has he mounted an unmanned horse.

"But pops- "Crystal protested.

"No buts Crystal. We'll be back soon." He gave Mistral a nod to get going.

"Stay right on my tail, I will be move fast," Mistral said, taking off at a sprint into the forest. Mistral, Captain Ruhk, Dame Eclipse, Duke Hardloff, Count Aldéric, and Sir Yuri rode off into the woods after Tiara and Chasten who were taken to the castle.

Chapter XXVI

Trophies

Captain Clod and his men marched through the dilapidated city and into the castle.

In the throne room, Captain Clod and Mayor Tomwell joined the Siren and King Tentaclous celebrating the capture of Tiara. Everyone had a smile except King Tentaclous who seemed to be disappointed.

"General, you have delivered us the key the renegades were waiting for," King Tentaclous said with a mug of mead in his hand.

"General?" Clod asked.

"After this last accomplishment, I'm promoting you. She must have been heavily guarded and you've lost so few men," the King said as he gulped down a few swigs of mead.

"She had just arrived and her armies were still gathering. It was a brief opportunity I exploited," General Clod said with a satisfied nod.

"After they see their 'Hope' destroyed, they should be easily defeated," Siren said confidently.

"What if they fight to get her back?" General Clod asked.

"They have strong magic on their side. They could revive her," said the Siren after taking a second to think.

"We need to end her in such a way so they can't revive her?" General Clod asked, rubbing his head.

"Yes, if we accomplish that, they would go back to squabbling amongst themselves," said the Siren.

"And Mayor Tomwell, your betrayal has worked out better than anyone would have dreamed," King Tentaclous said looking at the frightened Mayor.

"For a reward... perhaps I could be moved up to, say, a Duke or Marquis?" Mayor Tomwell asked greedily.

"I will give you knighthood," King Tentaclous declared with a wave of his hand.

"Knighthood? Is that all?" Mayor Tomwell asked with his hands out.

"You scoff at my gift? To be named one of my knights is a great honor. I'll give you nothing!" King Tentaclous said, slamming his mug down.

"N-no, sir. No, I don't. Thank you," Mayor Tomwell said, shaking.

"Good. General Clod without your actions, there would have been a great battle. Which some of us may not have made it out," King Tentaclous said with a sigh of disappointment.

"That is true, it would have been a great battle. Possibly the greatest battle of our age," General Clod said. The Siren looked at the General with a raised eyebrow. Clod was deep in thought.

"I can't help but think we should make this battle happen anyway?" he said thinking out loud.

"What?" King Tentaclous asked with a smile.

"We are barbarians. War is the lifeblood of our people," General Clod said with a proud nod.

"It's better not to let it go to chance," said the Siren. "Don't forget, we still have no way to deal with that dragon."

"You have magic, don't you?" snapped Clod. He turned to King Tentaclous, "My Lord, you are king of the barbarians. You are war itself. You are the epitome of what man and steel can do on a battlefield."

"That's right," King Tentaclous said, looking out toward the doors.

"Yes, but-" protested the Siren.

"I am the Barbarian King!" King Tentaclous shouted angrily.

"Release the queen, my lord, and let the next greatest battle come. It will define this entire land for eons to come," General Clod said with a clenched fist.

"Our victory will be absolute!" said King Tentaclous.

They could see a small amount of fear in the Siren's eyes.

"Wait! Think of how many of your men will die in battle. What if you die? Making a battle of this size happen is careless and reckless. Only a fool would give them back their key to victory!" pleaded the Siren.

"Perhaps you are right. But without her, it may not even be worth putting my armor on." King Tentaclous paused. "Everyone out, I need some time to think."

"As you wish" General Clod said

The room emptied. General Clod turned left down a series of long hallways, quickly putting an end to all the guards on his way. He then walked down a flight of stairs into the dusky, damp dungeon. Prison cells lined the walls, most of them full.

One cell contained two prisoners and a moldy old skeleton. Singing echoed down the passage and General Clod moved closer to the door.

"Breakin rocks in the hot sun, I fought the law and the law won, I fought the law and the law won," Chasten sang playfully.

"Will you stop that?" Tiara said in frustration.

"Yeah sure," Chasten said with a shrug of his shoulders.

"I can't believe I just froze like that," Tiara said, dropping her head into her hands in obvious frustration.

"Yeah, well, first time I fought some barbarians, I did the same thing," Chasten said with a quick nod of his head.

"But at least you charged in and tried something. I just stood there. I might as well have waved to him and said hi."

"I got caught as well," Chasten mumbled.

"I've failed all those people," she muttered in despair. "Why did you rush in like that? I mean, I know you're a hero but you were all alone?"

"Yeah well, I didn't exactly think it through. Plus, I um, love you." Chasten said in a muffled voice.

"What?" Tiara asked.

"I love you" Chasten said, embarrassed.

"Oh, I see," Tiara said.

An awkward silence filled the room for a second.

General Clod raised an eyebrow as he watched them.

"You think that skeleton could pick the locks on our chains?" Chasten asked to break the tension.

"Yeah I do, that's why he's still there as a skeleton," Tiara said sarcastically.

"Ok, well, he could take his arms off to get out and put them back on then come over and pull on your chains," Chasten said.

"True, and together we might be strong enough to break us out," Tiara said with a nod and a quick shifting of her hands to make them ready for a spell.

"You're a good sorceress; you could just make strengthen him, right?" Chasten asked.

"Uh, he has no muscles to strengthen," she pointed out.

"Oh, yeah."

"Hold on. *Orior spiritus os.*" A green mist grew in the skeleton's ribcage, its eye sockets started to glow neon green along with his ribcage area.and then the skeleton began to move and flicker with life.

"Skeleton, free yourself from those bonds and then free us," Tiara said.

"Yes, please," Chasten added.

Amused enough, General Clod broke open the door to the cell and Tiara and Chasten fell silent. He slowly walked toward them and then spoke to Chasten, "In the battlefield, you blocked my attack with your shield. Next time, duck and use your sword to parry my attack. Then hit me with your shield to push me off balance."

"Thanks, I think," Chasten said, surprised.

General Clod yanked on their chains, pulling them straight out the wall.

"You're quite strong," Chasten said in surprise.

General Clod nodded at him and quickly motioned his head in the door's direction, signaling them to go.

"Wait, what about me?" the skeleton asked as he got himself free.

The three of them looked at each other questioningly and Chasten just shrugged his shoulders. The four of them ran down the hallway and put a servant's entrance into the city. Once outside, the group was confronted by two guards, but General Clod didn't hesitate in easily and quickly knocking them out before they could shout for help.

"Go straight into the woods and you'll be able to find your way back from there," General Clod said, pointing with his sword.

"Wait, you're not coming with us?" Tiara asked still in a fog.

"I only want the greatest battle this kingdom will ever see to happen. You'd better hightail it," General Clod said as he turned around and started to walk away.

Tiara smirked as the skeleton and Chasten look at each other, confused.

"Well, thanks," she said. "Let's go." She turned and started to run as fast as they could for the forest line.

"So is he with us now?" Chasten asked.

"No, he's with Tentaclous. He just wants to fight us," Tiara huffing as they ran. The three of them soon disappeared into the woods and almost immediately ran into Captain Ruhk and the others.

"Tiara, Chasten, you're alive," Captain Ruhk said, surprised. "And free, how?" He raised an eyebrow.

"It's a long story and we need to get back so we can plan our assault," Tiara said.

"Did he help?" Captain Ruhk pointed at the skeleton.

"Yeah, he's with us," Chasten said quickly.

"Of course," shrugged the Captain. "Let's get out of here." Captain Ruhk extended his hand to Tiara and pulled her onto his horse with him. Chasten climbed up behind Sir Yuri and the group turned and headed back to Krylon.

General Clod ran into the throne room breathing heavily. Seeing him barge in, the Siren and her cronies followed.

"Sir, the prisoners have escaped. I tried to stop them but she used her magic," General Clod said, trying to catch his breath.

"We should have killed her when we had the chance!" the Siren shouted in frustration.

King Tentaclous slammed his hand down on a nearby table, breaking it in half. Then he paused for a moment.

"What are your orders?" General Clod asked.

King Tentaclous looked at General Clod, "We need to make preparations for the final battle." General Clod held back a smile. "You said she escaped using her magic?"

General Clod nodded, still trying to catch his breath. The Siren looked at the King and then at General Clod, a suspicion forming in her mind.

She realized what really happened. "What's wrong?" Mudmucker asked as he was right behind the Siren. "The queen has escaped" Siren said quickly as if snipping at Mudmucker.

"I guess we underestimated the strength of her magic," King Tentaclous said with a sigh and a smirk.

"Indeed, I saw a skeleton following her. She must know the forbidden magical arts," General Clod said still pretending to be worried.

King Tentaclous stopped and looked at General Clod with a confident smile.

"Indeed. I will investigate our security failings at a later date." The King grabbed a map of the city and placed it on the war table.

"As you wish," General Clod said with a humble bow and an arm across his waist.

"For now, we have a battle to plan. Awaken the army, get everyone ready for battle! I want all the officers in this room, now! Go!" King Tentaclous barked.

"Yes, milord," replied the Siren and General Clod in unison.

As everyone left the throne room, running to get the troops ready and already shouting orders, King Tentaclous walked to the corner of the room and pulled out a scroll with the map of the kingdom on it. He pulled a fresh table to the center of the room and unrolled the map on top.

Chapter XXVII

Clod's Mistake?

C rystal, Amy and Triskelon saw the party emerge from the trees and ran toward them.

"You guys are back!" Crystal yelled.

"And so soon?" Amy asked, surprised as to why the mission went so quickly from one of the most heavily guarded places in the kingdom.

"Chasten! Good to see you again, buddy!" Triskelon said welcoming his friend with open arms.

"Yeah, you too." Chasten said, tired and eager to relax for a while.

The two heroes hugged, jumping up and down with excitement like long-lost brothers. Captain Ruhk chuckled.

Tiara dismounted and gave Crystal a hug, and they walked into the centre of the town.

"Man, I thought you were done for," Triskelon said when they let go of each other.

"It will take more than an army of barbarians to stop us," Chasten said with a playful punch to Triskleon's shoulder.

"Amy, fight for me and I'll make sure they drop all the charges against you," Tiara said.

"Done," said Amy, and the two girls hugged.

"Captain Ruhk, do you have a map of the area?" Tiara asked, already wanting to prepare for the battle ahead of them.

"Yes, milady, right here. Count Alderic, hand it over," Captain Ruhk said holding out a hand.

"Sure thing, Duke Hardloff hand it over," Count Alderic said with a smirk.

"Absolutely, Dame Eclipse, you still have it?" Duke Hardloff asked with a chuckle.

"Yup, sure do. Chasten, where is the map?" Dame Eclipse asked.

"Yeah it's, er, here. I know it is, somewhere, wait. Here it is!" Chasten said, suddenly relieved.

He pulled the map from inside his armor and handed it to Tiara. She led the group into the town hall and up the stairs to Mayor Tomwell's office.

"Kind of exciting, isn't it?" Tiara whispered to Crystal, hoping she didn't sound as nervous as she felt.

"I'd say it's more nerve-racking. This will be a big battle. And those barbarians are huge, look at the size of their leader!"

"He wasn't their leader, just the guy in charge. I can't imagine how big their leader is," Tiara said, a lump starting to form in her throat.

She swiped everything from Mayor Tomwell's desk, leaving it clear enough for her to roll out the map of the kingdom and pin down the corners.

The group gathered around the desk.

"I'll attack from this side and-" Captain Ruhk said before being interrupted by Tiara.

"Excuse me," interrupted Tiara. "I believe I'm the one who's supposed to be in charge of this uprising."

"Excuse me, my lady, but it would be wise to let us handle the war. It's no place for a young girl," Count Alderic said with a small laugh.

"Tiara is better trained than you could hope to learn in 20 life times." Tarragon stated.

"I'm the Queen, Count, and I would remind you to not forget it. I'll be part of planning the battle and fighting in the war. If you don't like it, leave." Tiara scolded. Captain Ruhk held back a smile at Count Alderic's reprimand.

"Captain Ruhk, will you lead the assault on the castle's front gate?" Tiara asked.

"Absolutely," Captain Ruhk replied, happy to see that Tiara could handle herself.

"Maybe I should do that," suggested Crystal. "The Captain isn't as young as he used to be," she said in a low voice to Tiara.

"I heard that!"

"Maybe you should come in with the reinforcements," Crystal suggested.

"You can take the dog out of the fight but you can't take the fight out of the dog," Dame Eclipse said with a small smile.

Duke Hardloff, Captain Ruhk, Sir Yuri and Tarragon all laughed.

"Good, we will need everyone we can get" Tiara said. Dame Eclipse and Duke Hardloff, Count Alderic, I want you to attack the main gate head on with Alderic's, Hardloff's footmen. Mistral, Amy you however have another mission with Alderic's archers. Sir Yuri I want you to wait and only charge in when the time is right." Tiara said pointing out that they did not repair the damage to the gates.

"You want everyone to just attack the main gate?" Dame Eclipse asked.

"Doesn't seem very tactical," muttered Count Alderic.

"We're too small to attack different sides. We have to break through and kill Clod and King Tentaclous," Tiara said.

"Right we kill those two and the other half a million barbarians in his army." Duke Hardloff said in a relaxed tone.

"We shouldn't divide our forces. And don't you think the barbarians will fight for the sake of fighting? We might all die before we even get to the castle," Count Alderic said worried about his archers.

"Yeah they might, but if we can work together, we can do this," Chasten said, confident in the people who surrounded him.

"He's right, Sir Yuri's knights and Tarragon weren't even in the last battle," Triskelon said.

"They outnumbered us 3 to 1 before. I suspect their numbers have grown," Count Alderic replied.

"Yes, but our armies were scattered all over. Now, we're all here. And a direct attack isn't something they'll be expecting,"

Captain Ruhk said with a scratch of his chin as he stared at the map.

"I hope you're right."

"My city was recently sieged. We destroyed at least 1 of the King's battle groups," Duke Hardloff said proudly.

"Here, at this hill. This is where King Tentaclous will to try and take it. If he does, his forces will attack us from behind. That would be our downfall. All we need to do is keep them occupied until we have won the main battle," Tiara said pointing out the hill on the map.

"I agree," Duke Hardloff said.

"Tarragon and I will take care of the towers, Tentaclous is bound to have archers there. Once that's done, the army can charge for the main gate," Tiara said, solving one problem.

"I'll try to think of something," Tarragon said simply.

"Chasten, Triskelon, and Crystal. I need you guys to distract the towers, draw fire away from me and Tarragon. Take the skeleton with you. Trisk, you know a bit of magic, I'll teach you a stronger fireball spell." Tiara said having a back-up plan.

"All right, big fire!" Triskelon teased playfully.

"What about me? I can help," Mistral whispered in a half teary eyed voice because he thought she had forgotten about him.

"I have the perfect job for you and, who else is left?"

"Me," Amy said with her arms crossed.

"Amy, Mistral it's up to you two to maintain this hill. That hill is extremely important; if we lose it, we lose the fight. It's up you too and Alderic's army of archers," Tiara said with a confident smile.

"My archers won't follow her," Count Alderic said with a quick dismissal.

"They will if they wish to live past tomorrow," Tiara said quickly.

"I'll do my best," Amy said with a deep breath.

"Just follow your instincts, you'll be fine. I've seen you in battle. Mistral, I 'm counting on you as well."

"We will defend that hill with our lives," Mistral said, puffing out his chest.

"Good, I'm glad to hear it. You'll be out numbered, so don't just stand in the middle and try to fight them head to head. Distance and dancing around is your key."

"Have we missed anything?" asked Tiara.

"The Pirates from The Lost Harbor will cut off the supply lines from the sea. Admiral Stevens leads the way with a ton of effort to Eclipse." Ruhk said pointing to the sailing path on the map.

After a moment, everyone shook their heads.

"Great, we attack tomorrow."

They all left to prepare for themselves and their armies for what was to come. Only Triskelon, Chasten, Crystal and Tiara were still the Mayor's office.

"Tiara, it's not my place to disagree with you, but Amy is too young. Don't let her fight," Crystal said.

"If she can evade an entire army for as long as she did and still be strong enough to fight the both of us, she'll be fine. She's stronger than she looks, and she has wolf's instincts that will take over when she's in battle. We also don't have much of a choice, we need her," Tiara said in a tired voice.

"We need wolf's instincts in order to win the battle?" Triskelon asked.

"Wolves hunt in pacts, Trisk. They also slowly pick apart their prey one piece at a time and wear them out," Tiara whispered.

"Oh, I get it and the archers are the wolves," Chasten said with a smile. Crystal just raised her eyebrow.

The four of them left the town hall to see Captain Ruhk and Sir Yuri had made a fire in the middle of the town square and were now dragging old tree trunks into place so they had somewhere to sit. Tarragon was curled up to one side, back in his dragon form, and Amy and Mistral were playfully wrestling.

Suddenly Amy pinned Mistral to the ground and laughed.

"I beat the big bad wolf," Amy teased.

"Get off, I let you win. I didn't want to knock your confidence ahead of tomorrow," Mistral said with a smirk.

"Sure."

Amy let Mistral up, the two of them panting slightly from the exertion.

Chasten and Crystal walked over and joined them, sitting against one of the makeshift tree benches.

By now it was nighttime and the moon and stars had come out.

There wasn't a cloud in the night sky. Tiara walked off alone, politely excusing herself from the group and motioning for Triskelon to follow her.

"Ok, Triskelon when you're casting spells and you know the words but not the hand motions required, you can still cast the spell, you just have to touch your target," Tiara explained.

"Touch your target?" Triskelon asked.

"Yeah, with your hand. Instead of casting the fireball spell with one hand, hold your hands farther apart and facing each other, like this. Then circle your hands in the area you want the fireball to be. You must say the spell a few more times, but that should strengthen it. Use the word *frigus* and you can do the same with ice," Tiara said.

"Ok, thanks, I think I've got it," Triskelon said practicing the new hand movements to create a larger fireball, thinking about all the new spells he could translate that lesson into.

"There you go," Tiara said. "You can go sit down," she added after a moment of silence between them.

Triskelon turned to leave and Tiara started to whisper a spell that caused a white light appeared in her hands.

"What are you doing?" Triskelon asked like a nosy dog noticing the light.

Concentrating hard, Tiara squeezed it down to a small orb, and created a glass cover to contain it.

"Giving Amy and Mistral a secret weapon, just as a last resort sort of thing," Tiara said.

"What is it?" Triskelon asked curiously.

"I'd rather not say, it's kind of a gamble," Tiara said with a hint of nervousness. They went back to where the others were at and Tiara tossed the orb to Amy.

"Amy, catch," she said.

"What is it?" Amy asked.

"A last resort, use it when the time is right," Tiara said and bit her lower lip.

"When will that be?" Amy asked, studying the orb.

"Feel it out, you'll know when. Just throw it up into the air then have one of your archers shoot it," Tiara said, knowing that her needing to use that was inevitable.

"Ok." Amy replied.

Triskelon leaned over to Chasten and whispered, "Dude, Tiara just showed me how to cast any size fireball or ice ball I want."

"No way," Chasten whispered back, impressed.

"Yeah, watch this," Triskelon said and then cleared his throat. He placed his hands six inches apart and swirled them around just as Tiara had shown him. Then he called out the word for ice in the magic tongue.

"*Frigus!*" Triskelon said loudly and a ball of snow appeared in his hands. He playfully tossed it at Crystal.

"Hey! What was that for?" Crystal asked, narrowing of her eyes.

"I..." Triskelon began, then paused. "I thought I'd try to teach you how to fight before the war tomorrow." Triskelon teased.

"Oh, really?" Crystal said confidently as she slowly stood up and dusted herself off.

She suddenly leaped forward, grabbing Triskelon and forcing them to roll backwards. She easily pinned Triskelon to the ground and began gently slapping his face over and over.

"Hey, hey, hey!" Triskelon struggled to get Crystal off him whilst she kept slapping him.

Chasten looked over to where Tiara sat. She was gazing into the campfire and playfully letting the flames dance across her palms. Chasten tried to say something but nothing came out. Amy looked at Chasten and saw him looking at Tiara.

"Hey, skeleton, can you come over here a second? I want to see something," Amy said getting up and gesturing for the skeleton to follow.

"Sure," the skeleton replied and followed her.

"Skeleton I was curious, can you feel it when I do this" she asked and then slapped the skeleton across his skull. Skeleton stopped and stared at Amy in disbelief.

"No actually, I didn't feel that at all," Skeleton said sarcastically.

"Really?" Amy said as her jaw dropped she focused in some to stare at the skeleton.

"Of course I felt it! Let me slap you!" Skeleton said angrily.

"Ah" Amy said with a shrug of her shoulders. Amy turned halfway and playfully pushed the skeleton and then ran, who was soon followed by the skeleton. Chasten, Tiara and Mistral still sat by the campfire in silence.

"So, Tiara, what kind of things can you do with magic?" Chasten asked.

"I can do almost anything," she replied.

"Can you make the color of the fire turn blue?"

Tiara nodded.

"Nut uh," Chasten said.

Tiara turned the palms of her hands toward the fire and concentrated. "*Incendia puteulanus*," she mumbled.

"Wow," Chasten whispered as the flames began to change to a deep blue from the bottom up.

"All right, I have a challenge for you," Mistral said. "Let's see a green fire." Mistral said just picking a color that wasn't normally a fire color.

"I thought you said a challenge?" Tiara teased. She turned back to the fire and said, "*Incendia viridis.*"

The fire started to change again, this time from blue to green from the bottom upward.

"Wow," Mistral said gazing at the fire.

"Ok, let's see how good you really are. Let's see something really impossible," Chasten said. After a moment's thought, he suggested, "Cold-fire. Make Cold-fire."

"Cold-fire? Hmmm," Tiara thought for a moment.

"Good one," said Mistral with a smirk. "Let's see that Ms. fantastic at magic."

After finding the right words, Tiara once again turned her palms towards the fire. "*Incendia frigus incendia,*" she said. The fire turned white and began to give off a chill instead of warmth.

"Wow, feels like it should be snowing," Mistral said impressed. Tiara gave a quick flick of the wrist and the fire turned back to a normal.

"Oh yeah, I'm good," Tiara said with a smirk and a playful dance while still in her seat.

"How do you know so much about magic?" Chasten asked. "Triskelon messes around sometimes but he never casts anything powerful."

"Tarragon's has been teaching me magic since I was a child. It's all I know," Tiara said with a shrug of her shoulders.

"I'm going to call it a night," Mistral said, curling by the fire, his tail tucked around his body.

"Yeah, we have a long day tomorrow; I guess I'll call it a night too," Tiara said with a yawn.

"It's about that time," Chasten said, trying to put off going to bed just yet.

Tiara stood up and looked around the town. Then she placed a hand in the fire and slowly removed it, the fire dancing across her skin. She faced her palm down and made a rectangular motion. As the fire left her hand and spread out on the ground, it cooled and solidified into a small bed roll.

"That's an easy way to carry around a bedroll," Chasten said with a chuckle.

"Yeah, you want one?" Tiara asked as she lay down.

"Nah, that's all right, I'm used to sleeping outside by now." Chasten said trying to sound tough. As Chasten got comfortable, Crystal and Triskelon walked over and sat down. Tiara quickly makes him a bed, anyway.

"You guys are going to sleep out here?" Crystal asked.

"Yeah, why?" Chasten said.

"Why not just use one of the houses around here? I'm sure someone's got an extra room," Triskelon said with a shrug.

"I'm not rooming with those traitors. You can trust them if you want to, but I'm not," Tiara replied.

"Good point," Crystal said lying down near Tiara whilst Triskelon cuddled up next to Mistral.

Chapter XXVIII

Tentaclous's Battle Plan

Inside the throne room, King Tentaclous, General Clod, the Siren, Mudmucker, Grunting, Noctremis and Sir Mayor Tomwell stood around a map of the kingdom.

"They will not wait. They'll attack tomorrow. So, there isn't any time to prep the battlefield. I want our spearmen and crossbowmen in the towers that surround our gate. Siren you're in charge. Make your plan for the dragon when he comes," King Tentaclous said. Immediately after everyone gathered around the table, he had most of the plan in his head already.

"I'll look up some spells," the Siren said as she left the room with haste.

"This hill," King Tentaclous said, pointing to the map. "It gives us a clear path around their forces. It's that hill right there." He pointed to the same hill out the window. Which was the same window that Tiara and the others had planned for.

"How do you know they will be there?" Sir Tomwell asked.

"It has the highest elevation. And they won't be able to organize anything else that quickly. I want the four of you to take the forces the Siren gathered and take over that hill," he said, gesturing to Tomwell, Noctremis, Mudmucker and Grunting. "After that, circle around and attack their forces from behind."

"Force them to defend on both sides," General Clod said as he understood the King's plan.

"Exactly. General, you and I will be in charge of the ground forces around the castle. I'll wait inside. You're in charge of our defense until then," King Tentaclous said with a smile.

"With pleasure, my lord," General Clod said with a confident nod.

"Good, you have your assignments, now go get ready. After tomorrow everyone will finally understand that my rule is absolute!"

"All right boys, let's go. You heard the king," Sir Tomwell said, hurrying the other three from the room.

"Do you think they will attack the towers first? That Siren will be the first one down," General Clod said now that they were alone.

"Yes, that is a chance. Her only purpose in the battle is to take down the dragon. We can handle the rest. You think those idiots will take over the hill?" King Tentaclous asked with a chuckle and a shake of his head.

"No. Perhaps we should destroy the docks?" General Clod suggested.

"The only ships left are pirates. Not even worth our effort. I'll send a few troops to man the ships that guard our ports. That will be enough. The more that stand in defiance against us, the greater the victory."

The Siren looked through a book. She turned the pages in frustration. She muttered inaudible thoughts to herself. Then suddenly she stopped at one page, her eyes widened and her jaw dropped. "Siphon Strength, the dragon's power will be mine" Siren said as she finally had a way to get the power she craved for so long.

Chapter XXIX

Pirates Attack by Seaside

The day finally came and all the pieces of the final battle were falling into place one piece at a time. The fluttering of sails in the wind could be heard in the early morning sunrise. A fleet of ships sailed around the coast toward the King's castle. Men ran around frantically as Admiral Stevens barked commands at his crew. Most of the ships were together behind Admiral Stevens's ship, one ship however could be seen way out in front of all the others.

"Ready the port side cannons! Prepare to raise our flag!" Admiral Stevens shouted, unsheathing his sword and waving it around.

Cannons began to slide into view.

The coast was on their port side the barbarian ships; they were fast coming in to range and were largely outnumbered by the pirate fleet. "Whose ship is that?" Admiral Stevens asked as he looked to a ship with black sails out in front of all the others. The captain of that black massed ship had a compass that didn't point north along with a motley crew of misfits that sailed with him. "Drink up me hearties yo ho" He sang as he prepared his men to battle and loot whatever they could from the castle.

The ship with black sails sailed around the enemy craftily sailing through the blockade of barbarian ships. The other ships clashed and cannons roared while barbarians howled. Smoke covered the small harbor as the sea battle clashed. The cannon balls ploughed against the aged castle wall and the through the enemy ships.

"Incoming," yelled a barbarian seaman.

Aboard Admiral Stevens ship, barbarians and pirates fought hand to hand on the deck. The first moment Admiral Stevens got he pulled out his pocket watch and checked the time.

"We need to hurry. The battle on the mainland will start soon. Fight on ya scurvy dogs. On this day we will be remembered for all time!"

The sound of cannon fire turned to ships sinking and breaking apart from the waves. Suddenly out of the smoke bursted Admiral Stevens ships and a few other battle worn ships. Each of the ships were badly damaged and moving slowly towards the coast.

"Bring out the oars we will have to row to make it in time." Admiral Stevens shouted.

The sea battle was short but decisive as the pirates turned and sailed toward the castle. By the time they made it to shore the battle was happening already. Eventually the pirates manage to join the fight.

Chapter XXX

The Hill Battle

A t Mayor Tomwell's former town, everyone was busy. The town buzzed with activity. Duke Hardloff, Count Alderic, Dame Eclipse, Sir Yuri and Captain Ruhk were grouped together and getting ready to march out of the town.

"Years ago, when you fled the castle before, you said the king exiled you, us. Were you ever mad at him?" Crystal asked as she hugged her dad goodbye.

"At first, yeah I was angry. I wanted to fight with my men. Recently, however, it had occurred to me that the king gave me a gift," he replied, letting her go.

"What gift?" Crystal asked.

"Time. Time enough to see you grow into the woman you have become."

"I love you, pops," Crystal said holding back a tear and throwing her arms around Captain Ruhk's neck. Captain Ruhk hugged her back.

"I love you too, baby doll. See you on the front," he said, giving one last emotional squeeze before letting go. He climbed up onto his horse and made ready with the others.

"I'll see you on the field, Captain," Crystal shouted after him. Then Captain Ruhk turned to give her a final wave before riding into the woods, followed by the others.

Crystal joined Chasten, Triskelon and the Skeleton as they made final preparations. Silence enveloped all of them, and a slight nervousness was in the surrounding air.

"We ready?" Chasten asked, but no one replied.

"Yeah, I guess so," Triskelon said eventually.

Crystal took a deep breath and nodded as the four of them walked to their horses.

Tiara placed magical translucent armor on herself and Tarragon. Toward the center of each piece of armor was white like that of an ice cube. Tiara climbed onto Tarragon's back and gave him a pat.

"Ok, remember, I told Captain Ruhk that we'll only attack when they charge onto the battlefield," Tiara said.

"I was hoping for that. I want to fly really slowly," Tarragon said with a chuckle.

"Yeah, until the battle starts save your strength," Tiara said.

Tarragon took off, beating his wings as they ambled over the trees and disappeared into the distance. On the other side of the camp Amy and Mistral stood with the army of archers.

"This way, right?" she asked, scanning the forest.

"Yes, we should hurry and try to get to the hill before the barbarians do," Mistral said as he broke into a run, motioning for the archers to follow him. "On the double men, it's up to us to hold the hill," Mistral yelled over his shoulder.

Amy, Mistral and the archers ran into the woods, jumping over fallen trees and ducking tree limbs from time to time. Finally, they came out of the thick forest into a clearing where the hill stood. It was empty. Amy, Mistral and the archers slowly crept out of the woods.

"Good, we beat Tentaclous's men here," Amy said, her weapons ready.

"Quiet, we don't want to give away our position" Mistral said, ready to run back into the woods.

"We're sitting out in the open here; I think we already gave our position away," Amy said sarcastically.

"Charge!" Sir Tomwell yelled.

On the other side of the clearing, Sir Tomwell, Mudmucker, Noctremis, the Grunting and their barbarian forces charged up the hill toward them.

"They're here!" Amy yelled, momentarily freezing.

"Half of you with me, the other half with Amy, to both sides of the forest, hurry!" Mistral yelled as he and half the archers ran to one side of the woods. The other half disappearing with Amy on the other side. They disappeared into the lush greenery of the forest floor.

"On my mark," Amy whispered as the barbarians reached the top of the hill.

"We've won without even fighting," Sir Tomwell laughed, placing his hands on both sides of his hips and standing proudly on top of the hill.

"No, they are still here," Grunting said with a lick of his lips and a quick glance around.

"Now!" Amy shouted, and the archers stepped from the trees to let loose a volley of arrows.

"They're over there, get em!" Sir Tomwell yelled as the barbarians charged toward Amy and her archers in a chaotic mess.

"Into the forest," Amy shouted.

Amy and her archers jumped back into the forest and crouched down quietly.

"Follow me, stay low, stay quiet," Amy said. They crept through the woods and around to the other side of the hill, Amy in front, leading with her wolf-like movements and nose.

"Stop, they want us to follow them in there. Everyone stop," Mudmucker yelled unknowingly falling into the trap he was trying to stay out of.

"They want us to not follow them. Let's go in," Noctremis argued.

"What?" the Grunting asked, puzzled.

"They want us to go in. The forest is where they can hide," Mudmucker said in reply while staying low to the ground.

"Right, so what do we do?" Noctremis asked.

"Besides retreat?" Grunting asked.

"Interesting" Mistral pondered for a moment and then realized Amy's plan. "That is a good plan. Let's go" Mistral said as he motioned for them to follow. Before the cronies could get any further, Mistral and his archers jumped out of the tree line, took two shots and then jumped back into the forest.

"They're over there now!" Mudmucker yelled. The barbarians turned and charged toward Mistral and his archers.

"All right, let's go," Mistral said crouching low and moving with haste to another spot in the forest.

"Wait, now they will jump out from that side, so let's run and head them off," Grunting said, pointing to a new part of the forest and moving toward it.

"Let's just run into the woods," Noctremis suggested.

Mistral and his archers moved around the forest line and jumped out from another spot, forcing the barbarians to turn and run toward them.

Amy and her archers jumped out from the opposite side, causing even more confusion and forcing the barbarians to run around in circles.

"Reeeeet, they are everywhere," Grunting yelled out in frustration.

"This whole thing is a trap," Mudmucker panicked.

"Let's get out of here," Sir Tomwell said like a rat trying to desert a sinking ship.

"Enough of this, everyone into the woods," Noctremis finally shouted.

Sir Tomwell, Grunting, Mudmucker, Noctremis and what was left of their army all ran into the woods, ploughing through and knocking over some forest greenery.

As they ran into the forest, they came face-to-face with Amy and her archers. She paused for a second, and then smiled and waved, "Oh, hi," she said. Then, "Scramble!"

Amy and her archers ran out of the forest, trying to get away from the barbarians but they charged after them. The barbarians slowly closed the distance between them until the barbarians were in melee range of Amy's archers.

"You can't escape child," Mudmucker yelled.

"Our wrath is eminent," Noctremis added.

Mistral saw Amy running from the woods, with the barbarians close behind.

"We're going hand to hand. Let's go!" Mistral shouted.

Mistral and his archers jumped out of the woods, firing arrows at the barbarians. A few barbarians fell but it was getting increasingly difficult to get a clean shot as the bloodthirsty barbarians charged toward their prey.

"They're gaining on us." yelled an archer.

"We can't outrun them," yelled another.

Amy pulled out a small dagger and dropped her bow.

"Attack!" she yelled as Mistral and his archers ran into the battle. Turning to face the barbarian onslaught, many archers dropped their bow and took out their daggers whilst others used their bows to block the barbarian attacks but most tried to use speed to dodge each swing.

Amy found herself face-to-face with the Grunting who swung wildly and without finesse. Amy ducked and dodged as well as she could. She lunged in between each swing, making small cuts with her dagger but doing no real damage.

Suddenly a barbarian smashed into her, sending her tumbling down the hill. She sat up, semi-dazed, and looked at the surrounding battle. Her archers couldn't hold them off and she could sense the barbarian victory. Getting to her feet, and readying herself to re-enter the battle, she remembered the orb that Tiara had made her. She pulled it out and looked at it.

"As a last resort," Amy said under her breath. "I need you to shoot this," she shouted to a nearby archer, holding the orb up for him to see. He notched an arrow in his bow and gave a single nod. Amy tossed the orb as high as she could into the air. The archer quickly took aim and easily hit it with his arrow.

The orb exploded, turning the sky as dark as night. The sun faded away and the white part of the orb rose up, growing until it was the size of a full moon. Amy gazed up to the moon and began to shake. Amy transformed into a werewolf.

"Oh mama," Mistral said, taking a second to look around.

Moments later and Amy was in her werewolf form. Mistral took one look at her before charged back into battle. Mistral jumped and bit down on Noctremis's arm, digging his claws into him and knocking him over.

"Ahhh! It's on me!" Noctremis yelled in pain.

"I got him," Mudmucker shouted, running over to Noctremis. The Mudmucker took a swing at Mistral, only to be tackled by Amy. But not before taking out some of her own archers. She frantically clawing and biting Mudmucker like a wild beast.

Mistral then looked up to see Sir Tomwell trying to sneak out of the battle. Mistral sprung up and ran toward him, clamping his teeth around Tomwell's leg.

"Stop wolf, stop!" Sir Tomwell pleaded, gripping his leg in agony.

Mistral released his grip and pinned Tomwell to the ground with his front paws. "Trying to run? Traitor," he spat and said while pulling him back to the battle.

"Tentaclous will reign supreme," Sir Tomwell called out feebly.

"Tiara will restore order to the kingdom," Mistral said and then bit down again, this time swinging his head back and forth, tearing Tomwell's leg open with his teeth.

"Still think the king's offer is better?" Mistral asked with a smile, his teeth dripping in Sir Tomwell's blood.

"You may have beaten me, freak. Rest assured, as we fight so does the king himself. His army has never been beaten. He will win," Sir Tomwell said as his breaths became heavy.

"Perhaps, but you will not be around to find out," Mistral said with a final growl. He leaped forward and bit down on Sir Tomwell's neck, quickly ending his life.

"Sir Tomwell is down," Grunting said, seeing Mistral leave Tomwell's body and rejoin the fight. Seeing Amy tearing barbarians to shreds.

"So am I," Mudmucker shouted, hardly able to move.

"That means we're in charge," Noctremis said, wincing in pain.

"Sound the retreat," Mudmucker yelled trying to desperately crawl away from the battle.

"No, we are winning," Grunting said after looking at both armies.

"Three out of four of our leaders are down," Noctremis said now nursing his wounds.

"Yeah, but their numbers are dropping," Grunting declared, trying to renew their vigor.

"Time's up, run!" Mudmucker shouted with his final breath before collapsing.

"What?" Grunting said still fighting.

"He said, retreat," Noctremis yelled, hopping away from the battle. Grunting turned around, and started to run, the barbarians following close behind. The archers watched them go, dropping their weapons in relief. Amy ran halfway up the hill and stopped to watch them retreat.

Mistral sat down and panted heavily.

"Good thing they retreated, they were actually winning. Yea, we had their leaders down but look around only a few of us are left standing," Mistral said as he panted.

Amy turned around and looked at Mistral and the archers.

"A-Amy?" Mistral said, suddenly aware of the dangerous situation they were in. "You remember me, don't you, kid? You know, your friendly talking wolf? Your bestest buddy in the whole wide world?" Mistral asked trying to jog her rage blurred memory. Then, no longer in control of herself, Amy charged toward Mistral and the archers.

"Don't shoot her. Knock her out," Mistral commanded. He waited until Amy was within reach and then leaped forward, knocking her over. The two wrestled and rolled around and fought until finally Amy pinned Mistral to the ground. A flicker of fear passed over Mistral's face and then Amy went limp, collapsing on top of him. Mistral rolled her body off him to see a young archer standing nearby with a good-sized rock. Mistral let out a sigh of relief.

"Let's get our wounded. I have Amy; we need to hurry to the castle. We can put our wounded a safe distance away then we can enter the other battle. They'll need all the help they can get," Mistral said. Mistral picked up Amy gently and started to carry her, as the archers picked up their wounded allies. They all wearily walked into the woods, tired from the previous battle. Eventually they came to the castle where the battle was already happening.

Chapter XXXI

The Great Battle

eanwhile, as the hill battle happened Captain Ruhk,
Dame Eclipse, Duke Hardloff, Count Alderic, and
Sir Yuri were all at the forest line in straight out
from the front gate. The Siren was on top of one tower that
lined the city wall along with the Spearmen and Javelin throw-
ers she was now in command of.

"Count Alderic, what kind of armor are you wearing?" Sir
Yuri asked looking over the Count's shiny, unused armor.

"It was a gift from my wife. She insisted I wear it. After
she saw the state of my previous armor," Count Alderic said and
adjusted himself briefly.

"That wasn't the armor I gave you, was it?" Captain
Ruhk asked.

"It was, I kept it in good condition. It is still use-able,"
Count Alderic said after a quick shrug of his shoulders.

"It's going on ten years old," Captain Ruhk said with a
laugh.

"I became accustomed to it," Count Alderic replied with
a smile.

"Yeah, I've been using this old ball n chain for a long time now," Dame Eclipse admitted.

"I have a lucky cloth, tucked into my arm brace," Sir Yuri said as he pulled it out.

"I have nothing like that," Captain Ruhk said.

"Oh bologna," Duke Hardloff said with a loud laugh.

"I gave my good luck charm to my daughter," Captain Ruhk said looking up to the sky.

"What was it?" Duke Hardloff asked.

"The royal pendent and Dame Eclipse gave her the sword of the first king," Captain Ruhk admitted and a silence came over them.

"I thought that had been lost a long time ago," Count Alderic said.

"I saw your daughter give the sword to the queen this morning. Just before they left," Dame Eclipse said.

"Thanks to Dame Eclipse, it's been kept safe all these years. Now my daughter takes care of it. Or the queen, I guess," Captain Ruhk said.

The group appeared at the forest line in front of the city's main gate. General Clod stood inside the castle boundaries with his army, watching them.

Nobody moved.

"Well, they are still here," Captain Ruhk said, slightly amused.

"Did you expect them to leave?" Dame Eclipse asked as she unhooked her ball and chain.

"You can only hope," Captain Ruhk said with a shrug of his shoulders and a soft chuckle.

"Doesn't seem to be so many of them," Duke Hardloff said.

Crystal, Chasten, Triskelon and the skeleton were still sheltering in the trees on the other side of the battlefield watching the others appear and stand in front of the city gates, with a good view of the towers that surrounded the city.

"How long do you think it'll be until we will have to take over for Tiara and Tarragon?" Crystal asked, fidgeting on her horse.

"You plan on them failing?" Chasten asked.

"I try to plan for the worst, hope for the best," Crystal replied.

"Can you please go stand next to Crystal, you're freaking me out," Triskelon said, glancing over to the skeleton.

"The skeleton is freaking you out? What about the 2 kagillion barbarians waiting to kill us?" Chasten asked, looking toward the imposing towers.

"Seriously, they have half an army on those towers; I bet Tiara wasn't planning on that," said Crystal, starting to feel uneasy. "Look." She pointed to the soldiers lining the top of one of the towers. "That's not a barbarian. Whatever it is, it looks like it knows magic," she said, quickly trying to form her own plan in her head.

"Those spearmen probably won't do too much damage. But that *thing* will," Chasten said, looking to where Crystal pointed.

"Well, it's a good thing Tiara has shown me how to cast stronger spells," Triskelon said confidently.

"Yeah, how can we target the towers?" Crystal asked.

"There has to be a way up. We can break open the door and charge up the stairs. I'll go first with my shield, and you guys duck behind me," Chasten stated with a half-laugh.

"That's a sound plan for now," Triskelon replied.

"Why don't I go first and draw their fire, less on you guys," skeleton said with a shrug of his shoulders.

"We may need your sword up there. You're not expendable." Crystal said adjusting herself in her seat.

"If only we had enough time to make some catapults," skeleton said reluctantly.

"That would make things easier," Crystal replied.

"No use in worrying about that now," Chasten added.

"I hate this waiting around. I'm only getting more nervous," Crystal complained, looking to the sky for Tiara and Tarragon.

"You're nervous? I can't even hold my sword straight," Chasten admitted.

Suddenly, and without warning, Tarragon and Tiara flew past the tree line and soared high into the air. Everyone sprang into action.

The spearmen in the towers threw countless spears toward Tiara and Tarragon, forcing Tarragon to duck and dive to avoid them. With a deep breath, Tarragon swooped in and blew flames over a group of spearmen defending the leftmost tower. Screams could be heard as the spearmen caught fire and jumped off the tower to try to put themselves out.

Tiara concentrated on the gate which was down at the moment.

"*Directus*," Tiara said and the front gate to the castle began to rise.

"Concentrate on the dragon and its rider," screamed the Siren as she prepared a spell.

"*Incendia,*" the Siren said, summoning a fire ball and throwing it at Tiara who deflected it with an ice ball and aimed another at the Siren. The Siren and a few spearmen quickly jumped to one side only just dodging the attack.

General Clod watched the gate rise and took a deep breath. "Here we go," he muttered.

"It's opening by itself," said one barbarian.

Captain Ruhk and the others charged onto the field toward the castle.

Meanwhile, Captain Ruhk and the others charged past the city gate and into the cobbled courtyard.

"Don't let them through the gate! Squeeze them into submission!" General Clod ordered his men.

Captain Ruhk and his forces clashed against the barbarian army.

Already General Clod was losing ground. Captain Ruhk quickly turned to Sir Yuri and his knights.

"I need you to cut a path through," Captain Ruhk yelled to Sir Yuri.

"Aye, that's the sign." Sir Yuri unsheathed his sword and raised it up in the air. "Maintain formation," he ordered as he kicked his horse and led his knights into the battle.

In a tight V formation, Sir Yuri and his knights forced their way through the barbarian lines. Captain Ruhk and his forces soon followed behind, letting the rest of the rebellion forces past the gate.

Chaos ensued, barbarians and rebellion fighters were everywhere in the ruined city. General Clod charged into the fray, laughing as he made his way to Captain Ruhk.

"You, I remember you," said Captain Ruhk, coming face-to-face with Clod and spitting on the ground by his feet. "You almost killed me and my daughter." he said with narrowed eyes.

"Now you return so I can finish the job," General Clod said with a smirk.

"I've been waiting years for this moment," Captain Ruhk said, tightening his grip on his sword and shield.

"Pity it will be so short," General Clod replied. Clod lifted his sword for the first swing as Captain Ruhk dodged the blow.

Cannons could be heard from the other side of the city and shouts rang out, "Pirates, our ships have fallen!"

Suddenly, the sky turned dark as night and a strange full moon appeared. Tarragon feinted to the right, trying to desperately dodge the spears being thrown at him.

"What is going on?" Tarragon shouted.

"Amy must be in trouble," Tiara replied, deflecting the Siren's bolt of lightning.

"Should we go help her?" Tarragon asked.

"I have my hands full at the moment. We can't, but don't worry, I gave her a secret weapon," Tiara said.

Crystal, Chasten, Triskelon and the skeleton watched as Tarragon weaved through the sky and Tiara threw her own spells back at the Siren and the spearmen on the towers.

"That's it, we've waited long enough, lets rock," Crystal said, unsheathing her sword and motioning for her small force of troops to follow. They charged toward the city gate but just as they entered the city, there was a terrible scream from the sky.

They heard the Siren yell out *"Tribuo Potentia"* Crystal turned back to see a magical rope being thrown from the tower. It entangled Tarragon, wrapped around his wings and caused him to crash to the ground. The black rope snaked its way up to the Siren's hands, up her arms and into her chest, connecting her to Tarragon.

Crystal frantically looked for Tiara on the ground, but she couldn't see her. Looking back to the Siren, she watched as her skin turned black with an evil glow. Then the Siren began to morph into a huge black dragon.

"Tiara's down, we have to protect her," Crystal shouted to their small group.

Clinging to the tower's walls, the Siren let out an almighty roar and a breath of fire into the darkened sky.

"That thing is killing Tarragon, we need to cut it somehow," Triskelon shouted.

"I have an idea" Chasten replied.

Chasten charged toward the rope and, with his sword in both hands, swung as hard as he could at the rope. His sword bounced off the rope and sent him a stumbling back. Triskelon quickly summoned a fireball and shot it toward the rope but it had no effect.

The Siren spread her wings and launched herself off the tower, heading for the battlefield, breathing fire as she went.

Crystal grabbed Tiara's sword and swung at the rope in desperation. It sliced through easily, and fell away from Tarragon's body, crumbling to dust. A painful shriek echoed across the battlefield and the black dragon turned mid-air and headed straight toward them.

"Form a circle around Tiara until she comes to," Crystal shouted to her troops. The soldiers bustled together, shoulder to shoulder, forming a protective ring and readying themselves to face the dragon. The skeleton joined them but was ripped apart when an axe blew out his chest and sends the skeleton to pieces.

Chasten ran over to Tarragon as he wearily stood up, weakened from his sudden loss of strength.

"All right, buddy, you need to take out the other dragon," Chasten said, pointing to the Siren.

"I'll try, protecting Tiara," Tarragon replied stumbling slightly as he got to his feet and spread his wings.

"Don't worry about us," Triskelon shouted, charging back to Tiara and the others.

"You got it. Don't worry, we'll help you take out that dragon," Chasten said.

"How?" Triskelon asked.

"I have no idea." Chasten replied.

Chasten and Triskelon ran over to Crystal and joined the circle around Tiara. Tarragon took a few steps, flapped his wings and took off into the sky, flying toward the Siren. The two clashed on top of the city wall like two lions that fought for dominance. They swung, clawed and bit each other violently.

The Siren swung her claw at the weakened Tarragon, and crushed her claw against the side of his head, forcing him off balance and revealed his neck. The Siren lunged forwards before Tarragon could regain his balance and bit down on his neck. Tarragon yelled out in pain before slumping over the city wall, his tail hitting the ground near to where Crystal and the others stood. Tarragon tried to get back up but collapsed, his breathing heavy as his wound turning the wall blood red.

"Tarragon is down," Chasten yelled out in fear.

"Let's go!" Triskelon shouted, casting a few fireball spells to clear the way.

"We're coming!" Chasten shouted.

They ran toward the two dragons and just as the Siren was about to deliver the final blow, a fireball hit her squarely in the side of the head. She turned toward the two heroes, snapping at them viciously with her new razor sharp dragon teeth. She swung her claw at them, thumping it down on the ground, forcing Chasten to roll forward as Triskelon rolled backward. Getting to their feet, they ran up Tarragon's tail and onto his body still slumped over the city wall. Chasten swung his sword. The Siren snapped at him and then tried to swipe him with a claw. Chasten blocked the attack with his shield, forcing him backwards.

"I'm going to enjoy eating you," the Siren snarled. She took a deep breath and let out a stream of fire. Triskelon jumped behind Chasten and they both crouched behind his shield for protection. The Siren's fire surrounded them; the shield just barely kept them alive and was already red with heat.

"No!" Crystal yelled out as she watched in horror and tears sprang to her eyes.

"The shield is melting," Chasten shouted. Triskelon patted his friend on the shoulder.

"*Eternus Vir!*" they yelled together. "*Vivat Regina!*" They yelled again.

"We gave her a hell of a run buddy," Chasten said as the metal on his shield began to drip onto the ground and onto his arm. "I can't hold this much longer," he said through gritted teeth, struggling against the sheer force of the fire.

"I have an idea! *Frigus,*" Triskelon said with a smile.

Ice formed around Triskelon's hands. He reached forward and touched Chastens shield. It began to burn his hands and Triskelon could feel the panic rising.

"*Frigus,*" he said again, this time louder. His hand started to cool and then the shield slowly became encased in ice.

"Ha-ha. It worked!" Chasten shouted.

"Gotta love a long shot!" Triskelon laughed in reply.

She snarled and then let out another breath of fire.

"Ice my sword, I've got an idea," Chasten said, adjusting his arm.

Tiara slowly came to as Crystal gently patted her face. "Come on, Tiara. We need you," she muttered. Seeing Tiara's eyelids flutter, she let out a sigh of relief. They both looked over to the Siren and saw a bright blue iced shield in the middle of the fire.

"Tiara, look," Crystal said happy that the two in the fire were still alive. Tiara blinked a few times to focus and then got to her feet.

Tiara and Crystal watched as a frozen sword appeared out of the fire. Then then threw it toward the Siren.

Thinking quickly, Tiara began to cast a spell, "By the power of the light, that sword will fly straight and true! *Volare prorsus et verus*," she said, pointing one arm toward the royal pendent and the other toward the iced sword.

The sword flew toward the Siren and buried itself deep in her chest. The Siren screamed in pain and slowly began to transform back into her original form. She took a few steps backward and finally fell onto her back. Chasten stumbled forward, his hands still red, grabbed his sword, and then followed Triskelon down Tarragon's tail and back to the ground. They ran back to the group, jumping and whooping in delight.

Captain Ruhk picked his strikes carefully; using his agility against the big, brutish General Clod used his strength. Each attack that General Clod swung was a hard blow, Captain Ruhk used it against him, dodging in and out as best he could, but he was tiring.

Dame Eclipse joined the battle and swung at General Clod's head, but he ducked and parried her attack then swung back at her, hitting her square in the chest. Dame Eclipse fell to the ground. His attack just barely pierced her armor and cut her chest. The wind was knocked out of her. Soon Duke Hardloff, Count Alderic and Sir Yuri joined in against General Clod as well, they took turns while the other was knocked back.

General Clod openly took them all on and blocked each of their attacks and stepped in between them as he used his position and continued the fight. One by one Duke Hardloff,

Count Alderic, Dame Eclipse and Sir Yuri were all wounded. General Clod however swung his weapon with all his barbarian might and tried to fight them all off still.

General Clod and Captain Ruhk clashed in the middle of the battle.

Mistral, Amy and their archers appeared at the forest line and watched Captain Ruhk take Dame Eclipse's place as he charged at General Clod.

"Those of you who can still fight, follow me," Mistral shouted. He turned to the unconscious Amy still in her werewolf form under the fake full moon and licked her face. Amy woke up and started to growl at Mistral.

"Come on, sleepyhead, we've got work to do," Mistral said with one last teasing lick and then he turned and ran toward the castle.

Amy charged after him and they both entered the battle.

"Mistral, Amy, you guys made it," Tiara yelled out waving a hand to catch their attention whilst she thrust back at an injured barbarian.

"Thank the gods," Crystal said with a breath of relief.

"Careful," Mistral said as he charged past them.

Tiara saw Amy come barreling into the fray, swinging at anyone who stood in her way.

"Oh no," she said.

Amy came closer and then swung at Tiara, but Tiara was able to move quickly enough to dodge the attack. Avoiding the thrashing about of sharp claws, Tiara put a hand on Amy and said, "*Imperium versi pellis.*"

Amy took another swing, forcing Tiara to let go.

"Watch it, she isn't in control," Mistral shouted.

"At least she's a good fighter," Crystal said, trying to hold the line.

"Hang on!" Tiara said. She put her hand on Amy once more and said, "*Ego Gubernere.*"

Amy suddenly stumbled. She looked everyone around her and then down to her fur covered body.

"Oh, my G- "

"We need you," Tiara shouted, turning back to the fighting and defending herself against a charging barbarian with a spear.

Amy didn't reply, instead she ran into the fray ripping apart barbarians as she went.

Inside the throne room the sound of metal crushing the marble floor could be heard. Iron footsteps walking out to the balcony that overlooked the battlefield nearly shook the very ground.

"Abbigonians!" A voice rumbled, echoing in every corner.

For a moment, a silence descended over the battlefield. Everyone looked to the balcony attached to the throne room where King Tentaclous stood dressed in his suit of armor.

He drew out two battle axes and shouted, "Fight for your survival."

Then, the king jumped off his balcony and landed on the battlefield. The ground shook and the stone where he landed cracked like a spider web. The king charged toward the battlefield and everyone leaped back into action with renewed vigor.

"There he is," Tiara shouted slowly fighting toward him.

"This ends now," Chasten said.

Chasten, Triskelon, Tiara and Crystal charged through the few barbarians between them and the king. Tiara and Triskelon both launched fireballs as Chasten, and Crystal lunged with their swords. Mistral and Amy soon joined them, fighting to keep barbarians from interrupting their fight. The King blocked and dodged their attacks with ease. Tiara launched another fireball as Crystal thrust forward, leaving her left side open. King Tentaclous broke through her defenses and used her own weight to smash her against the castle wall, cracking her chest plate. Lifting his axe, he tried to swing only to receive a fireball to the shoulder which knocked him off balance.

Turning toward his attacker, his eyes fell on Tiara.

"You," then charged toward her.

Chasten saw this and charged as well. Tiara continued to cast as many fireballs and lightning spells as she could but King Tentaclous shrugged them off, grimacing from the pain as each one hit him. He lunged forward, thrusting his axe toward Tiara when suddenly Chasten pushed her out of the way, taking the blow himself.

The King's axe broke through Chasten's armor and buried itself deep into Chasten's chest. Chasten fell onto his back. Tiara's eyes welled up as she got up and hovered over Chasten. Crystal and the others only watched Tiara as Tiara stood over Chasten.

"My queen, I love you" Chasten said holding his hands over his wound.

"Chasten, no!" Tiara screamed as Chasten fell onto his back. Triskelon ran to his friend but Tiara remained rooted to the spot. She clenched her fists and growled in anger.

Smokes erupted from her eyes and very skin itself as the barbarian troops started to step away from her and toward the other people in the battle. Then fire burst into flame.

"Tiara," Crystal shouted and threw the sword of the first king before bending down and scooping up a discarded barbarian weapon as a replacement.

Tiara caught the sword with her right hand and it to burst into flames, the fire flowing up the sword. Then she attacked King Tentaclous in a fit of rage

"Hey buddy," Triskelon said, holding his friend close. "I think she loves you," he said with a small laugh happy that they both have feelings for each other.

"How about that," Chasten said unenthusiastically, his breathing becoming labored.

"You know for a second I thought she was just going to heal you" Triskelon said with a smirk.

"one could have hoped" Chasten said with a deep breath.

"Let me get you fixed up." Triskelon snapped his fingers and the axe slowly removed itself. Triskelon then laid his hands on Chasten's chest and muttered a few different words as he tried to remember the healing spell.

"*Sanitatem*" Triskelon finally remembered and Chasten's wound started to close itself. Triskelon pulled his friend out of the fight and then rejoined the battle.

Tiara combined her magical abilities with close combat attacks to knock King Tentaclous back. She held a hand out in front of her then touched her side after she muttered each set of words.

"*Ceratotherium vis vires! Acinonyx jubatus velocitatem*," she said, strengthening herself, faster and with better armor.

"*Ferrum Cutis*," Triskelon said, adding to her array of spells.

Triskelon helped Tiara cast spells on herself as well. Tiara became as strong as a Rhinoceros and as fast as a Cheetah and Tiara's skin became like iron. She squared off against the King as King Tentaclous squared off against her. King Tentaclous swung his axe. Tiara ducked and punched King Tentaclous square in the stomach, but her hand only hit his armor. Then she swung at his feet with her sword forcing him to jump. Tiara's fighting style matched that of skill and rage, she used whatever she had at her disposal, Tentaclous smiled as her fighting style became like his own.

"This is my Kingdom!" King Tentaclous shouted in a rage. He swung back at Tiara and struck her wherever he could. Each strike of his sword cracked her armor.

Crystal helped Chasten back up onto his feet.

"I am the King of War! I will never be defeated by a weak little Abbigonian such as you," he shouted and continued to swing at Tiara hiding the fact that the thrill of battle that he hadn't had in years was slowly overcoming him.

"This kingdom's true queen has come for you, monster," Crystal shouted. Tentaclous growled heavily and clenched his sword against Tiara's and then shoved her back. She took a few steps back and fell on to her back as Tentaclous stood over her. She was surprised at Tentaclous's true strength. Even using magic she couldn't match his titanic unstoppable strength.

"I AM the true King," King Tentaclous shouted out loud.

"You will pay for every sin you have committed!" Tiara shouted. Jumping back to her feet. "Every honest life you've ended!" She parried the King's attacks, Tiara trying to make an opening for her to run the king through.

Their weapon's clashed and King Tentaclous smiled, thinking he had the upper hand.

"Not from the daughter of a deposed King and Queen" King Tentaclous said trying to make her more and more angry.

Just then Amy, Chasten, Triskelon, Mistral and Crystal jumped back into the fight. Amy dug one of her claws into king Tentaclous's side then Crystal thrust her sword into him. But King Tentaclous continued to fight as usual. Mistral Clamped down on King Tentaclous's calf thrusting his head back and forth against it and tearing it apart. Triskelon started to summon a very dense fireball. Then threw it toward the King, knocking him back. Tiara then jumped forward and grabbed her sword in a reverse grip and sunk her sword into King Tentaclous's chest. King Tentaclous took a few steps back and fell to his knees.

"This is my kingdom," King Tentaclous said in a labored breath. He grabbed the sword that stuck out of his chest and pulled it out. His blood seeped into the surrounding ground. He stepped one of his feet so that it was flat-footed but still kneeled. Then King Tentaclous fell to his back, lifeless.

"The King has fallen," Tiara shouted over the battle.

The clash of metal on metal began to die across the battlefield as the barbarians began to realize it was all over.

General Clod and Captain Ruhk continued to fight. General Clod swung his axe, knocking the sword from Captain Ruhk's hand. It clattered on the ground, too far away to reach. Clod swung again but Captain Ruhk dodged his attack with a roll to one side which in an instant picked up his sword and pierced his sword through General Clod's heart.

"How could I have been defeated by such small creatures?" he said in a final breath before falling backwards and lying amongst the dead bodies of his fellow barbarians. Everyone else on the battlefield stopped the fight and turned around to look at the fallen king.

Duke Hardloff stepped up with his sword and aimed it; suddenly stopped by Captain Ruhk. "He's gone" Captain Ruhk breathed. "The queen has returned. Long live the queen" Captain Ruhk shouted loudly and victoriously.

"Long live the queen," Dame Eclipse shouted.

"Long live the queen!" the others joined in.

"Long live the queen," the troops chanted.

Crystal ran through the crowd of those still alive and threw her arms around Captain Ruhk's neck.

"You're alive!" she said, relieved.

"It's going to take more than a barbarian General to take me out," he chuckled, hugging her back.

"We'll have to have a ceremony to crown you queen," Crystal said, turning to Tiara as the others approached, shaking hands with Dame Eclipse, Sir Yuri and Count Alderic.

"We don't need a ceremony, we need to rebuild," Tiara said dismissively.

"There must be a ceremony, my queen, it is a long-standing tradition," Count Alderic professed with pride.

"Very well then, let the ceremony begin" Tiara shouted with a smile toward Crystal.

"Give us a few days to clean up the throne room first," Captain Ruhk said as the troops shouted and cheered.

"Tend to our wounded," Tiara commanded. "Crystal, can you round up the remaining barbarians? Arrest them all and make sure they swear allegiance."

Crystal nodded, gathered a few soldiers and herded the last few barbarians into one group. Some tried to run into the forest but were quickly chased down by Mistral.

Tiara looked up as the moon exploded and sunlight returned, flooding the battlefield with light. The sky turned back into daylight just then the pirate captain of the black-sailed ship walked out of the castle littered with jewelry all over him. Admiral Stevens walked up from the other gate.

"So we won, excellent," said a voice. The group turned to see Admiral Stevens at the castle gate, draped in jewelry.

"And in a few days, we'll have a coronation," Captain Ruhk said, shaking hands with the Admiral.

"Oh, I love ceremonies! Drinks all around," laughed the pirate. Everyone stood around and talked. People started to fit back into their lives. Some people cleaned up, others mourned the fallen. Others laughed and tried to live to the fullest, greatful to those who had taken part in the battle that had just happened.

Chapter XXXII

Crowned!

L oud music filled the castle. The ruins and the fallen bodies of the battle had disappeared and the castle, and the city that surrounded it, looked new once again. People threw confetti into the streets and there was happiness in the air the city hadn't seen for years.

Captain Ruhk, Count Alderic, Duke Hardloff, Dame Eclipse and Sir Yuri waited in the city square whilst Dame Eclipse held the royal crown in her hands.

Crystal, Triskelon, Amy, Chasten and Mistral sat in the front row. Triskelon and Crystal held hands. Triskelon leaned over to Chasten and whispered, "You should make your move before she gets crowned. You will have to make an impression."

"Otherwise, she'll be queen and impossible to get," Amy whispered, leaning in on his other side.

"You think?" Chasten asked.

"Think how romantic it would be if you made your move before she gets crowned in front of everyone," Crystal said leaning across Triskelon to join the conversation.

"Just don't jump out and say hello," Amy said, with a playful rolling of her eyes.

"You need to be romantic. Quote some poetry or something," Triskelon said.

"What?" Chasten asked incredulously.

Crystal shook her head quickly and said, "Speak from your heart."

"Just be like, hey pretty mama. Let me give you a sniff," Mistral teased. Triskelon laughed.

"Don't say that either," Amy said, noticing how agitated Chasten was, and throwing a scowl toward Mistral.

"My heart isn't telling me to say anything" Chasten said sounding panicked.

"Stop freaking out, it's all right. I put in a good word for you," Amy said.

"You did?" Chasten asked, looking hopeful.

"No, I just thought that might calm you down," she replied with a giggle.

"Amy!" Chasten complained.

Just then people from the crowd started to shout and cheer and someone shouted, "Here comes the queen," and the cheering got louder.

"Running out of time hero, just do it," Amy encouraged.

Tiara walked down the open street. She shook hands with her people, hugged the women and kissed the babies. Slowly she made her way down to where Captain Ruhk and the others were.

"Ok, show time, hero. Remember, just speak from your heart," Crystal said with eager anticipation.

"Don't worry, I'm right behind you, buddy," Triskelon said with a tap on Chasten's shoulder.

"Thanks" Chasten replied.

Tiara walked up to where Captain Ruhk and the others were. She waved to Crystal and her friends in the front row. Triskelon nudged Chasten, and he slowly stood up. Tiara locked eyes with Chasten and smiled.

"Chas," Tiara said with a small smile as she waited awkwardly for him to say what she knew he was trying to say.

"Tiara, um hello," Chasten said. Amy buried her head into her palm with a smile and shook her head back and forth. Tiara saw Amy and laughed softly.

"Is something up?" she asked.

"Tiara, whenever I'm around you, I can't breathe. You're all I can think about," Chasten started to say.

"Aw," Crystal said, holding her hands up to her cheeks.

"I had way better lines when I romanced you," Triskelon whispered to Crystal.

"And what lines were those exactly?" Crystal whispered back.

"Ok there were no lines; I just had to teach you how to fight. It was difficult but..." he shrugged his shoulders.

"Oh, really?"

"Oh yeah well, you know..." Triskelon trailed off as Crystal rolled up one of her sleeves. Panicking, Triskelon jumped up behind Chasten, causing Chasten to jump at the sudden movement. Tiara covered her mouth and tried not to laugh. Crystal laughed.

"Don't worry buddy, I got your back," he said, patting Chasten on the shoulder. "What my friend is trying to say here is that he loves ya. In fact, he won't shut up about you," he said.

"Not sure this is helping," Chasten muttered from the corner of his mouth.

"Nah, you're golden," Triskelon said.

"Well, I haven't kissed her yet," Chasten said.

"What are you waiting for?" Triskelon shot back.

Chasten nervously took a step toward Tiara. They locked eyes for a moment and then he slowly reached forward and slid her hair back behind her ear. Tiara grabbed the front of his shirt and quickly pulled him to her, kissing him square on the lips. The surrounding crowd cheered as Chasten recovered from the shock and kissed her back.

They pulled apart, smiling at each other. Chasten sat back in his seat with a hard thump, dazed. Tiara turned and walked over to Captain Ruhk still smiling and kneeled. Dame Eclipse handed the crown to Captain Ruhk who then placed it onto Tiara's head.

"Rise a queen," Captain Ruhk said proudly.

Tiara stood up, and the crowd cheered again. She then walked over to the front row and stood before Crystal, drawing the sword of the first king from the sheath at her side.

"Crystal, take a knee," Tiara said with a smile.

Crystal looked at Triskelon, took a deep breath and then kneeled before her new queen. Tiara placed the blade of her sword on one of Crystal's shoulders.

"By the power vested in me by my parents the King and Queen of Abiggonia and the people of Abiggonia, I name you,

Dame Crystal," Tiara said and placed the sword on her other shoulder. "Rise a knight." as she finished speaking.

Crystal stood up and hugged Tiara.

Then Tiara turned and looked at Amy.

"Do you want to live with me in the castle?" she asked.

"I'd love to," Amy said without hesitation.

Tiara looked at Mistral who let out a small whine. "You can come too," she said with a chuckle and then glanced over to Count Alderic who was shaking his head. "You can lead my hounds," Tiara explained.

"Oh, yes, quite the responsibility," Count Alderic said. Mistral howled in excitement.

"Crystal, I will need a good knight at my side, would you like to be my personal adviser? You can bring your sidekick, too," Tiara said nodding toward Triskelon.

"I would be honored," Crystal said with a smile.

"Whoa, I'm no one's sidekick. Chasten and I are heroes," he said, and they both puffed out their chests, put their hands on their hips and looked out toward nothing.

"For once that's actually true," Crystal said with a laugh.

"Actually? We've saved the day thousands of times, right?" Chasten said glancing over to Triskelon.

"What? Sorry, I was in my hero stance," Triskelon said. Tiara and Crystal laughed and shook their heads.

"We should set a meeting sometime, Ruhk," Dame Eclipse said nudging Captain Ruhk as they watched their new queen.

"I'm thinking dinner," Captain Ruhk said with a smile.

"Sounds lovely." Dame Eclipse replied.

"Finally, we can have peace in the kingdom. The people will begin to rebuild everywhere," Captain Ruhk said with a wide gesture.

"Now we have to worry about the surrounding kingdoms," Dame Eclipse replied.

"Not now, for now, we all live happily ever after." Ruhk said with a smile.

The   End

Mark Peanut Three Accola

Mark went to school for Culinary Arts and Culinary Management. After getting into the industry he learned that it wasn't for him. He also worked construction for 9 years, working with his family in the family construction business. Mark and his brothers started a YouTube show called Peanut Gallery Review and earned the name Peanut Three. One day when he woke up, the idea randomly came to him to write a book, and then he wrote it. This book is the book he started with.